Shirley Wins

by Todd Taylor

D1248783

GORSKY PRESS
LOS ANGELES • CALIFORNIA
2006

Published by
Gorsky Press
P.O. Box 42024
Los Angeles, CA 90042

copyright © Gorsky Press, 2006
all rights reserved

ISBN 0-9753964-5-5

cover photograph
by Dan Monick

all illustrations
by Art Fuentes

cover design
by Sean Carswell

Dedicated to Marge Taylor

CHAPTER ONE
Pink Dots on the Horizon

Shirley and her granddaughter Rachel kept a low profile on the day of the pumpkin launching competition. They'd driven overnight and stayed off of the freeway, not sure how the cannon would weather being towed at more than fifty miles per hour and not sure how they'd respond to the questioning of a highway patrol officer if they were pulled over. They'd paid their twenty-dollar entrance fee, read a brochure about how launched pumpkins were great for fertilizer, and learned that a local farmer donated the use of his land for the weekend. The rules regarding the picking up of one's own trash were printed in all capitals, underlined three times.

Shirley carefully drove through the knotted throngs of people setting up their launchers, found the paper plate with her number on it, and backed the cannon into place. She was nervous. No one but Rachel had ever observed her in physics action. Rachel wasn't comfortable either. They sat in the car for over an hour and watched the sun get higher in the sky. It was still early. Shirley listened to one side of a Vangelis tape. Rachel had brought along her favorite Replacements album and was pleased when her grandma mouthed some of the words to "Favorite Thing." As the tape clicked to play the other side, Rachel ejected it from the player. "Ready?"

"I think so."

Their technique was tight and their methodology pushed back some of the fear they felt. Off came the tarp. Out came the level. Sights were adjusted. Slight wind was compensated for. The barrel was inspected and the bicycle was attached. Lawn chairs were set out. Binoculars were mounted.

"Let's get these pumpkins officialized," Shirley said.

Shirley and Rachel had fancied up the operations by putting all of the pumpkins into a little wagon and pulled them to the inspection station.

A man with hair like a lion's put one on the scale and marked the weight, to the tenth of a pound, with a black grease pencil. "Lumina?"

Shirley looked at Rachel, who looked back at Shirley.

"Pardon?"

"This pumpkin a lumina?"

"No, it's a white diamond," Rachel responded.

"Never heard of one of those. I gotta split one open. Make sure it's not made out of rubber." The man unsheathed a large knife from a holster on his belt, flicked its blade open, cut out a deep slice, and inspected it. "These'll work real nice. Gotta lot of meat on 'em."

"Thanks," Rachel said.

The man wiped the blade clean on the side of his pants then weighed all of their pumpkins.

"First time at the launch?" the man asked.

"Yes," Shirley answered guardedly.

"Sampson," the man said as he held out his hand. "Always glad to see new people launchin'."

As Shirley shook Sampson's hand, it felt like a lion's paw filled with restraint. He didn't crush her hand, but it was massive, the skin thick and rough. "Good luck. You square with all the rules?"

"Just one question."

"Shoot."

"Can anyone tell me how far away that old car is out there?"

"You mean the outhouse?" Sampson swiveled and pointed with the tip of his knife to an outhouse that was sitting on the flatbed of a rusted-out pickup truck out in the field. "That's about six hundred yards. As a matter of fact, that's the record running here. If no one can hit it, we'll drive it up into range and have a go at it. What you got shootin'?"

"No, no." Shirley replied. "The old car."

"Which one?"

"I think it's a Duster."

Sampson worked through his confusion and realized that Shirley was flirting with the highly improbable. Many of the rookie launchers did. "Shoot, ma'am, that came with the property. Some drunk ran it into a tree two days after he'd bought it new, and it died right there." Sampson looked up to study Shirley's face. The woman was serious, if not a little too ambitious. "I'm not quite sure I know. What you shootin'?"

Shirley pointed towards her cannon, blazing pink, even in the morning haze. Her face was blank. "Mind if I measure? I've got a wheel."

Sampson tried not to laugh and was largely successful at hiding his grin with his hand and faking a cough. He looked at his watch. Then he looked at Rachel's and Shirley's sweaters and realized that the two were color coordinated with their cannon. "Knock yourself out. Launching starts in a little over an hour. We try to get the competition throws in the morning before the wind picks up. Good thing you wore those sweaters. We'll be able to see you just fine."

Shirley and Rachel headed straight to the car, dropped off the marked pumpkins, picked up the measuring wheel, and counted its rotations. The car looked closer than it really was. Shirley made a notation and let out a full mouth of air in determination. "It's almost exactly half a mile."

"That's really far. Think you can do it?" Rachel asked.

"Can't see why not. Count with me back? Double check?"

"Sure."

When the two were out walking on the field, some of the curious stood back and inspected the pink cannon, like it was an exotic animal with a funny haircut on a short leash.

"Tassels? Those tassels on the bike handlebars? What kinda crap is that?" one man jeered.

"Pink paint?" another asked. "That don't seem right."

One man just repeated the word "pussified" over and over again.

"A bike?" Still another inquired.

And so it went, around and round the circle of men casting aspersions, except one or two quiet ones.

A man with a thick, long, waxed, and balanced moustache saw past the easy flash of skin and could see the kinetic inner workings, step by step, as plainly as if the cannon had a neon halo over it. "I'll be jiggered," he said. "That could do it. If it works like it should, it'll be divine." Many things, from the cannon's clean transfer of energy, to the obvious mastery of the welds, impressed him.

"Whose is this?" another man asked as he walked into the fold.

Fingers pointed out to the field, to the small dots of bright pink walking towards them.

The crowd dispersed the closer Shirley and Rachel got, willing to stand back and see what transpired. She could fail all on her own and never become a problem.

Shirley sat down with a calculator and punched in numbers. Although she didn't have to, she drew a chart. When she was done, she was still nervous, so she drew both her and Rachel as stick figures. That made her feel better.

CHAPTER TWO
The Puma of Physics

Shirley had had an affinity for physics in high school. Equations weren't abstract, one-dimensional codes that were just numbers on a slide rule, but living, four-dimensional explanations of light, time, weight, and probabilities. She could not only see the spine of the supporting math, but the flesh of its existence in the way water flowed out of a faucet, how airplanes flew overhead, to how bullets left the muzzles of guns. She imagined blueprints over anything she thought about for more than a few seconds—their trajectories were as clear as the gypsum lines between the bases on a baseball infield. These things filled her thoughts. Shirley even developed a slight crush on Sir Isaac Newton's brain. She didn't care for his hairstyle or the fact that he was long dead, but his ideas, well; those were sexy to Shirley. He explained what was invisible to most people. Shirley was very interested in that which people couldn't see but affected every step they took, every second of every day. Invisible things—like air, faith, and physics.

The infatuation with physics had started almost forty-five years prior, but life has a way of folding up what you really like, putting it in a garbage sack, hauling it to the local dump, and handing you a job in its place. The real world needs money to live in it. Shirley knew this and took it in stride. She was used to being considered average. In fact, she counted on it.

Most people never gave Shirley a second thought, which gave her considerable leeway on her side projects. Over forty years ago, she had become a secretary for the water district and slowly rose through its ranks, guarded by predictable pay and hours. Shirley's demeanor fit her job.

Her personality at work was like some Asian fighting technique she'd never heard of, based on self-defense and the avoidance of blows. She wasn't unfriendly, but people rarely came over to her house after work. She didn't go to many parties. Many of her coworkers didn't quite understand it, but when they talked to Shirley for any amount of time, they would eventually get the feeling that she wasn't invisible, rather she was holding up a mirror. It felt like they were talking to themselves when talking to Shirley. She mentioned almost nothing of her private life. Most people like talking to themselves and appreciate a good listener. About all her co-workers and bosses knew for sure about Shirley was that she liked to knit. A lot. When the holidays rolled around, everyone knew who knitted the excellent scarf for the secret Santa gift exchange. Shirley was thoughtful. A scarf is the only article of clothing that is truly one size fits all.

Shirley had met her ex-husband, Frank, at work. He worked in the field most of the time. His job required him to electroshock fish below hydroelectric dams. With long poles placed in the water, hooked up to an obscene, but carefully regulated amount of voltage, his job was to stun fish, and take their readings and measurements. After he jolted the water, the fish would just float to the surface. He'd scoop them out, and among other things, see if they'd been chewed up by the turbine intakes in the dam. He was away a lot—his work took him over much of the Northeast—and was like Shirley in many fundamental ways. By no means unfriendly, he still kept to himself. The two were like very weak magnets with the same polarities. They were often close but not quite touching. They also appreciated that they each needed their own time and space. They had divorced long ago, well before Rachel was born.

Rachel's mom, Willamena, had died delivering Rachel. Shirley was in the delivery room, holding her daughter's hand moments before the last pulses of life passed through her heart, before the hemorrhaging became unstoppable, and then Shirley was escorted out. Quickly thereafter, Rachel was placed against Shirley's chest, swaddled and wailing. Neither Shirley nor Rachel stopped crying for very long that first week. Rachel's father had left Willamena the day she'd told him she was pregnant, threw a hundred and fifty dollars on the bed, and told her to get an abortion. He went to get a cup of coffee and only came back once, in the middle of the night, to get his stuff when Willamena was at work.

From day one, Rachel looked almost-too-exactly like Willamena. Shirley knew what she had to do. Hit the reset button. Bury one child. Raise another one, twenty-two years after the first. The pain, frustration, and powerlessness of an unexpected death was slowly turned around and inside out with each new thing: a patch of dark brown hair that sprouted overnight, a new tooth, a first step, a first word. Although she never thought of her as a replacement, Shirley took great comfort in her grandchild, who had so much of the living spirit of Willamena. Shirley had a second chance. Maybe she could get Rachel to avoid a couple of Willamena's mistakes. Although she had to work beyond a normal retirement to support them both, Shirley harbored no lingering resentment, or felt that life had dealt her a raw deal. Rachel was a great kid, smart as all getout.

Shirley's resurgent interest in physics came benignly. As was her practice, after she parked at the supermarket, she walked to the closest abandoned grocery cart—so it wouldn't potentially damage any cars—and started pushing it into the store. One time, as she was about to plop her coupon caddy into the cart, she noticed a physics book in the top basket. She looked all around her. Nobody was looking like they'd lost anything. She flipped the book open. No school stamp. No student's or teacher's name. No library due date. She began skimming through the pages and was immediately flooded with memories of high school physics: equations, theories, and laws. They were like long-forgotten friends. Thermodynamics resonated so much more with her than who had been homecoming king and queen. After standing in the parking lot, rapt in reading for over half an hour, she pushed the cart into the supermarket and did her shopping. A fireworks display of physics was exploding in her mind.

That night, she pored over several chapters. Her imagination fizzed and popped with phosphorescent colors.

At work, she found herself doodling force versus mass equations. Like secret love notes she didn't want anyone else to see, at the end of the day she crumpled them up and tossed them in the trash at a nearby service station as she filled her station wagon up with gas. Months went by and she plowed through several volumes that she clandestinely checked out of the library and read before she went to sleep. Lying down on her bed at night, Shirley's ceiling filled with incandescent equations and formulas, swirling in vivid constellations above her, until she fell asleep.

One could assert that Shirley was addicted to clipping coupons, but addictions are bad things. She took an alphabetized card box chock full of potential savings with her every time she went to the supermarket and a good run would take twenty to thirty percent off of her total shopping bill. Certainly, coupons appealed to her frugality. But there was something more. Coupons were part and parcel of the testing grounds of what Americans would tolerate. Many times, coupons were for new products, products that manufacturers weren't quite sure would fly, products that needed a little extra push to see if it'd stick like a dart in the bull's eye of the collective brain of the consumer. Shirley wasn't impulsive. She steered clear of blue pudding. She was intrigued, but didn't bite at oatmeal, that when mixed with hot water, activated tiny dinosaurs out of egg-shaped marshmallow bits. Potato chips with riddles imprinted right on them patently creeped her out.

Shirley loved frozen lasagna. She'd fancy it up with some extra sauce and cheese of her own, and she'd try every new combination that came her way. One day, she hit the trifecta. The relaunching of an entire lasagna line. It was the exact same lasagnas that she knew and loved, but with different designs on the packaging. She couldn't lose. In fact, she thought to herself, all I can do is save. She ripped out the entire page, planning to cut it up during the final selection process when she would file the coupons into their appropriate subcategories.

Shirley was continuing through her ritual clipping of the Sunday paper when Rachel came in the front door, a gust of wind at her back. Small bits of paper scattered off of the kitchen table as Shirley made a corral with her forearms, flattening down most of them before they could flutter to the ground.

"Man, it's windy out there," Rachel said as she knelt down and picked up the clippings that had made it to the floor. She scooped them up and placed them back on the counter. "Get anything good?" she asked as she opened the refrigerator door, surveyed the contents, leaned on the door for several seconds, and then closed it.

"Am I old fashioned if I think that food shouldn't have writing on it?" Shirley asked.

"Like a label or a wrapper?"

"No, like writing right on the food."

"Like a brand on a steak?" Rachel shrugged. "I've only seen that in commercials though."

"On a potato chip," Shirley said. "It's a dye, I think."

"What's it say?"

"Different jokes, depending on the chip."

"No. You're not old fashioned. That's just wrong," Rachel replied, opened up the refrigerator again, bent down, and took out a can of soda. "I don't want to read my food. Even if it's funny."

Rachel walked off to her bedroom and Shirley started

organizing the scattered coupons. When she got to the lasagna coupon page—the only full page of the day—for no reason whatsoever, she turned it over before clipping it.

What first got her attention was the large, gaudily painted plaster trophy of what turned out to be—upon further inspection—a leprechaun holding a pumpkin above its head. The byline was "First Annual Pumpkin Chuck a Success." Shirley read the entire article, turned the page over, had her scissors at the ready, then turned it over again.

She read the article once more, this time slowly. Half of her brain was immediately cramming full of as many physics equations as she could remember. They crashed on top of one another, breaking apart messily, fluid spraying everywhere, in a car wreck-style pileup. The other half of Shirley's head filled up with this vague, but very real tugging and suction. She felt a little woozy.

Shirley was experienced in the coupon arts. She knew her supermarket wouldn't accept a photocopy of a coupon. She put off her final decision by gently folding up the page of the newspaper and placing it in the very first slot in her coupon caddy. If the call of the lasagna was too great when she passed it in the frozen food aisle, she could always crease the paper and tear the coupons out by hand at the last minute.

When she had the supermarket's refrigerator door open, the coldness continuing to cascade down the front of her, her hand feeling the icy weight of lasagna, she made her final decision.

True. She could have bought another newspaper and had both the lasagna and the article on pumpkin throwing, but Shirley felt that to give up something intentionally which she really liked was making a stand. Sure. It was a small stand, but it was an invisible line that she had crossed. Bathed in a wash of fluorescent light, she steeled herself that she was going to at least try something very dangerous and potentially embarrassing that made little sense beyond this: she just wanted to do it.

She bought a pumpkin pie in quiet celebration.

It was sometime during those months that a tiny, almost imperceptible seed germinated. She wanted to make some physics of her own. She wanted to build a machine that displayed physics that was as naked, transparent, and as powerful as its coveted laws. Not the cow of physics, but the puma of physics: sleek and muscular. She wanted to do more than just write love letters to physics. She wanted to do more than just hold its hand and do predictable, choreographed dance moves. She wanted it to hunt and stalk and lunge and feast. She wanted loud, gnashing, teeth-baring, satisfying physics.

Shirley rubbed her hands together as the plan clicked into place. It was at that moment she understood that she wanted to see if she could make a contraption that would launch a projectile and hit the old mill.

A broad, indefatigable smile spread across Shirley's face.

To make sure she wasn't selling future talents short, she put down her cup of cocoa, picked up a rock from her back yard, and threw it as hard as she could. She picked up three more rocks and threw them. Not one of them had made it to the mid-point of the ravine. The challenge she had set for herself was as palpable as the wet, hard rock in her hand.

Laughing, she raised a fist at the empty factory. "Arrgghh!" she yelled, sounding like one-quarter pirate and three-fourths homemaker. Then she went back to finishing her cocoa while devising a plan of attack.

CHAPTER THREE
The International Sign for Touchdown

At a medical supply store, Shirley purchased fifteen feet of surgical tubing. At home, she knitted a little pouch for the rocks to nestle in before launching.

In her backyard, she found that if she removed her gate, unscrewed the decorative horse heads that capped off the top of the six-feet-apart metal posts, and slid eight-feet-tall 2" x 2"s of wood into the holes, her catapult would be stable. The wood was snug. There wasn't a lot of play. With the wood in the metal posts, it looked like old-fashioned, but miniature, football goal posts.

She popped the 2" x 2"s out of the postholes. Wrapping pieces of thin leather around and around near the tops of the pieces of wood, Shirley strapped a spring-locking climbing carbine on each one. The surgical tubing was tied together so it was a big, loose "O," like a big mouth hanging open. Shirley snapped the tubing into the clasps, then slid the wood back into the metal posts. She centered the pouch, which dangled about a foot off the ground. Her contraption was basically a large slingshot.

Palms sweaty, Shirley picked up a rock, carefully nestled it in the pouch, and pulled back. The surgical tubing stretched and the wood flexed ever so slightly as she scooted several paces back. Not knowing how much stress she could put on the tubing or the wood and not wanting anything to break, she let go of the pouch before the tubing was completely taut. She fell on her butt as the rock snapped forward. It twirled and jiggled and twisted. The pouch Shirley had knitted was too soft and had wrapped around the rock. The force of momentum freed it on an unpredictable path.

The rock broke Shirley's kitchen window, smithereening the little porcelain dog dressed as an angel upon whose wings Shirley would place her rings so she wouldn't lose them down the drain when she washed dishes.

On her back, Shirley looked over to the new hole in her house. The shattering of the window had been very loud. "Crimeny, how'd it do that?" she whispered. It was at that time that Shirley got the idea of wearing a football helmet. Dusting her butt off, she walked over to where the window had been less than a minute before, and peered into her house. Besides shards of glass and the cracked wings and bits of head from an obliterated porcelain dog figurine, everything looked okay. The rock laid benignly at the foot of a large teddy bear.

Shirley surmised that her love of knitting had overshadowed the physics at hand. For a test, she loaded another rock into the pouch. She bobbled it. The rock moved easily. "It got stuck," she said as she continued to bobble it. "I've got to fix that." Shirley began to disassemble the equipment. She was in no hurry.

Luckily, it was morning and she had all day to go buy a replacement pane of glass and reinstall it. No one was any the wiser.

Shirley hadn't taken a sick day in four years, and, as it so happens when working for the government, she stumbled into "use it or lose it" days, where it didn't matter if she went to work or not, she'd still get paid and wouldn't be reprimanded. There was also a change in her department's policy. The three sick days per year she'd been accruing the last forty-odd years would not roll over to the next. Shirley had an unprecedented six weeks off, since at the end of her off days, the holidays began. Fortunately, she had a plan.

Shirley became bolder. After seeing Rachel off to school—she had taken to keeping all of her notes in a binder—and she would pore over them and redo bits of equations and refinements of diagrams. In accompaniment to the mental tai chi, she figured that a leather pouch was the way to go, and then made one heck of a sturdy rock pouch. She stitched a handle to the back of it.

She threaded the surgical tubing through the new pouch. The old pouch was already on its way to being re-worked into a tea cozy. Shirley stood at the edge of the ravine. Little wisps of white air puffed out of her mouth from the cold, through the grate of the football helmet. She clapped her hands together, warmed them up.

With the slingshot ready to go, she placed a rock in the pouch and pulled as far back as far as her muscles could take her. According to plan this time, she dropped. When her butt hit the ground, she released the pouch.

The rock's arc was true. Its actual trajectory was almost dead on to the blueprinted trajectory in Shirley's binder, which satisfied her to no end.

The rock landed on the far side of the ravine. It was still a good hundred yards more to the mill.

Shirley gave the international sign for touchdown, giggled, and clapped her hands. Her cheeks were cotton candy pink. She was happy. This was good. This was fun. This was vacation.

For the next half an hour, Shirley scavenged all the sizeable rocks out of her back yard, carefully placed them in the pouch, and launched rock after rock—about fifteen. All of them landed within twenty feet of each other. Each launch was logged into her notebook.

Her muscles began getting sore. Typing and being in front of a computer all day hadn't prepared Shirley's forearms and back for such a strain.

Knowing that accidents happen when fatigue sets in, Shirley stopped for the day. Shirley had barely enough energy to rend the wood out of the posts and put the gate back on its hinges. She was pooped.

She was already thinking of more improvements. She wanted to replace the wood supports with metal. She wanted to get more tubing. She wanted to get stronger.

At first, Rachel didn't notice anything changing in her grandma. Like everyone else, Shirley had her good days and her bad days, but Shirley's good days were on a championship-type run. Her grandma seemed content. It's not that Shirley was ever timid, but there was some sort of fire inside that Rachel was beginning to pick up on. Some sort of confidence. Some sort of action.

Shirley had become a master garage saler at a very early age. Shirley's mother, Wanda, swore that the third and fourth words out of little Shirley's mouth, after "Mama" and "Papa," were "garge" and "sale." Her mother had taken her on early-morning knick knack-strafing runs virtually every weekend morning for well over a decade. Shirley was well aware that "early birds," as they were called, had the well-deserved bad reputation of poaching the best stuff by haranguing the people holding the sales an hour before they could get all of their stuff out of the garage, but Shirley didn't think that bad manners ever had an excuse. She always waited for the garage sale to officially commence.

Industrious and a born multi-tasker, Shirley took to walking to the garage sales in search of slingshot improvement parts. With a carefully mapped-out route from all of the addresses she'd highlighted in the newspaper, a backpack, and a water bottle at the ready, she wanted to improve her cardiovascular system while walking to the sales. Keystrokes on a keyboard in front of a glowing box just weren't cutting it. She also began the habit of picking up appropriately sized rocks during her walks. She kept the first two rocks in her hands. She used them as weights. The rest she would put in the backpack, if it wasn't filled with garage sale loot.

At first, the garage sale routes were around a mile, with only one or two sales to stop at. But by the end of the month, Shirley clocked in a four-miler and came home with two fifteen-foot-long plumbing pipes.

Shirley began to feel defiant. Her arms were noticeably stronger from a month of successful launches—exactly 873 in total—and the pipes were the enhancements she was banking on. Twenty-eight days into her siege against the paper mill and she had yet to hit it.

Shirley wasn't quite sure why she hadn't told Rachel what she was up to. Maybe it was because she wasn't convinced that it was a good idea to be mucking around with a giant slingshot. Maybe it was because she wanted to have something all her own. Maybe it was because she didn't want her granddaughter to look down on her, although Rachel, for all intents and purposes, was a good kid whose only vices were loud music, questionable haircuts, makeup that extended to all corners of her face, and ripped up clothes. Maybe, Shirley thought, I'm just being plain silly.

The pipes slid into the fence posts like pistons in the cylinders of a racecar: perfect fit, absolutely no wiggling. Shirley's thoughts of Rachel dissolved then congealed around the situation at hand. With the clasps fastened, the surgical tubing without any kinks, and the now softened leather pouch at the ready, Shirley strapped on her helmet, squeezed her hands into fists, pumped them up and down several times, and said in her personal pep talk voice, "The time is now. You've got it today, Shirl. You betcha."

She loaded a rock into the pouch, pulled the tubing back further than it'd ever gone, feeling the rigidity of the steel poles in her forearms, and let loose.

Although there couldn't have been fire trailing the rock, it looked like a meteor to Shirley. The rock actually hummed as it spun. It hit the side of the mill with a loud pthwap! Shirley did a little dance and high fived the air.

To make sure it wasn't a fluke, but a structural improvement, she quickly loaded another rock and launched it. Again, another satisfying dent and a distant, sharp, gongy sound. Shirley was addicted. She reloaded the slingshot.

CHAPTER FOUR
Sort of in Love with Physics

Rachel pedaled her bike up to the house. Being that she had to loop around the ravine on her way back from school, she'd been hearing thuds of indeterminate origin every minute or so for the past five minutes. She figured it was kids. After she put her bike in the garage and walked into an empty house in which her grandmother was usually easy to locate, she heard another not-so-distant thud. It was amplified and seemed to be coming from the back yard. She walked to the kitchen and looked through the window.

It was definitely her grandma. She was wearing her favorite sweater, but not much else made sense. A football helmet? A huge slingshot that was launching rocks at the paper mill?

Rachel was as patient as her grandmother and not one to jump to any conclusions.

She watched her grandma pick up another rock from what was apparently a bucket of rocks, place it in a pouch, rear back as far as possible, land on her ass, and let the rock fly. As she opened up the back door, the thud of the rock was louder. Her grandma looked funny in a football helmet.

"Grandma!" Rachel yelled.

Shirley, startled, looked around. Her mouth fumbled for words. "Hi... honey... how was school?"

"Grandma, what are you doing?"

"Are you out early?" Shirley, embarrassed, looked at her watch. School had gotten out a half-hour ago. She had lost track of time.

"Grandma, what are you doing?"

Shirley pursed her lips. She never lied to her granddaughter—not about periods, not about having sex, not about her gardening, not about drugs, not about how a girl wearing ripped fishnets gives off the wrong impression—but she had to hurdle herself over some initial hesitation. "Rache, I'm launching rocks at the paper mill," she said dumbly.

"I know. I just saw you."

"Oh, you did?" Shirley unsnapped the strap to the football helmet, took it off, and patted down her hair.

"It's pretty loud," Rachel said.

"I guess it is." Shirley smoothed out the front of her sweater. Shirley started a long speech with "Do you ever have these ideas in your head that you just want to get out?" And then she told the entire story about finding the physics book, her physics journal, the pumpkin chucking article, all of her equations, and ended it with "Well, with physics, I'm sort of in love with it. I want to see what I can do with it, but I don't want to neglect you."

Rachel smiled. The fire in her grandma's eyes was unmistakable. "Mind if I give it a shot? It looks fun."

Shirley was surprised and pleased at how well her explanation had gone. "Only if you wear the helmet."

Rachel hesitantly took the helmet and placed it over her head.

"It does no good if you don't strap it on," Shirley goaded. "Safety first."

Rachel softly puckered her lips and made sure the cup of the strap was firmly against her chin.

Shirley told Rachel the underlying ideas and after taking her through a dry run of the technique she'd developed, she handed Rachel a rock. "Take it easy the first time, just to see how it feels.

We've got plenty of rocks."

"I can see that. Damn, grandma, you don't mess around."

It was when Rachel was pulling back the pouch from the sides, not the specially made handle in the middle, that Shirley winced at her own lapse of instruction.

Rachel was a natural in the ballistic arts. She pulled back really far and fell flat on her butt. It was the uneven release that unleashed a little demon. The rock should have flown towards the paper mill, but because Rachel let go of the pouch unevenly, it arched viciously back towards Shirley instead. At first, Rachel was disappointed. She put a hand up to block the light coming into the helmet and looked out towards the paper mill. There wasn't the neat sound of a rock hitting it. Rachel also didn't hear the soft collapse of her grandmother.

Sitting up, before she looked towards her grandma, she asked, "What happened? I don't see where it went."

Shirley was on the ground. A large, expanding kiss of blood pooled through her sweat pants. The pain was colossal. Shirley's mouth pursed tightly. Her lips became white from the angry knots of pain. Tears streamed down her face. All she could mutter was her version of swearing. "Dang-butt, dang-butt, dang-butt."

Rachel screamed in fear when she put the sequence of events together—that she'd just probably crippled her grandmother —and she rushed towards her. Blood was all over Shirley's right shin. "Ohhh, grandma. I'm so sorry."

Shirley smiled weakly. Each word was labored and said through gritted teeth. "Honey… it's… okay… please… take… me… to… the… hospital… please…."

Horrified that she had just maimed her grandmother, Rachel rushed her to the emergency room. Rachel felt like throwing up, like someone had hit her with a rock, too.

On the ride to the hospital, Shirley felt the world collapse and get sucked into her shin. At least it felt that way. The pain was accelerated. It was blindingly hot and white and felt like all those years of sitting under fluorescent lights while doing cubicle work were being siphoned and funneled right through her leg and hot wired to her brain. It was the largest hit Shirley had ever taken in her life. The good news—although Shirley had no way of articulating it at the time as she groaned and shifted her weight from one side to the other in a sad two-step—was that the pain was like a bomb. It collapsed and obliterated the little subdivisions of half-formed obligations and commitments Shirley didn't really care about. It had been a dull, dispersed weight that was hard to recognize because it accumulated so slowly, over decades. Heck, no, she didn't want to be in the knitting group anymore. "I love to knit alone. There's nothing wrong with that," she whispered in a whine. She decided right then to quit the Knit Wits.

Rachel looked over and put a soft hand on her grandma's shoulder. "I'm sorry, grandma. You're going to be fine." Rachel hoped she wasn't lying. "We're almost there."

"The Chamber of Commerce: when's the last time they called me when they didn't need something?"

Rachel's just kept rubbing her grandmother's shoulder.

The pain was clarifying. It knocked out the clutter from the gutter and cleaned up Shirley's path of future activity. She wanted something to call her own. She wanted something big and pure and raging full of physics, not just a backyard slingshot that a child could build.

Shirley's brain began to feel chalky and crumbly. Her eyes lolled.

"Grandma! Grandma! Stay up!"

Instant spiderwebs of red veins skittered across Shirley's eyes as she jolted herself awake. "I'm here," Shirley rasped.

Rachel ran inside the emergency room.

She ran back out with two EMTs, one pushing a wheelchair.

Shirley smiled as they gingerly transferred her from the car, wincing whenever her leg moved. "Rache, you're a good kid. I love you, too." She raised her index finger for emphasis. "Don't you forget." Her finger curled slowly and her hand dropped as another wave of pain came crashing into her and sucked her into its undertow.

Luckily for Shirley, the doctor on duty wasn't afraid of giving his patients anesthetics. Within thirty minutes of being admitted, Shirley was knocked out cold. Her body relaxed. Her brain became as fresh and as uncomplicated as a chalkboard wiped by a clean, wet rag.

Luckily, too, it had been a simple fracture, not compound, and eight hours later, Shirley was back home in a brand new cast that covered up the biggest bruise she'd ever received. Her thoughts were muddy. It was no longer clear what had happened.

Shirley felt wickedly punched. She wasn't mad at her granddaughter. It hadn't been Rachel's fault—she knew that—and she'd told her that many times. In no small way, Shirley was happy that Rachel had accidentally turned her leg into a swollen, purple mass of damaged tissues and bruised bone. It made Shirley want to punch back at a slowly dissolving world—one that she hadn't even noticed was hobbling away from her before chancing upon the abandoned physics book in the supermarket parking lot.

CHAPTER FIVE
Bloody Knuckles and Bruised Confidence

Rachel's interest in gardening had budded early on in life. During spring and summer, fragrant flowers would bloom as bright as organic fireworks, next to beefmaster tomatoes and rows of cauliflower and carrots. Rachel's specialty, though, was pumpkins and squashes. Gardening had come naturally to her, ever since she started planting when she was six or seven. She'd made a hanging garden from an old clothes rack. Her summer squash would often look like obese, yellow balloons, ready to pop.

One summer, when Rachel was ten, the two of them stretched and stapled clear plastic over fence pickets and set up a rudimentary greenhouse that leaned against the rear of the house. Improvements came each season. The greenhouse grew larger and more sophisticated—as did the vegetables and flowers nurtured inside of it. By the time Rachel was fifteen, she had replaced the plastic sheeting with specialized glass and installed grow lights for the cooler temperatures. Even during the bitterest winter months, aromatic and beautiful lilacs, lavender, plumeria, and gardenias bloomed.

Like her grandma, Rachel had secret passions. It's not that she wasn't proud of her horticulture and flora—she was delighted—but she couldn't come up with any good reasons why she would boast to other people about her interests. Plus, it wasn't cool. It wasn't like she was playing in a punk band or secretly growing weed or doing something her classmates would easily understand or appreciate.

Beauty remained hidden in the back of the house.

Winter thawed. Spring came and went. Flowers bloomed like a spontaneous riot all around the house. Summer started.

Shirley's leg had healed, but she had a new worry. Shirley stared at her bloody knuckles. It wasn't only the physical pain that made her cry, it was shame. The simple shame of having some pretty darn good ideas, the best plans she could make at her fingertips, and it didn't mean diddly if she couldn't turn a screw into a piece of metal. Metal shavings from the stripped-out screw heads glistened brightly.

She'd done everything correctly. She'd pre-drilled a couple of holes into the metal frame, just a little smaller than the width of the screws themselves, so they'd fit snugly and hold. But after several twists, her screws would go off on slight angles and no matter how hard she tried to bring them back to true, all she was able to accomplish was stripping out their cross-topped heads, so she couldn't even unscrew them.

Her hands cramped and ached. They felt as useless as if her regular hands had been replaced with others permanently stuck inside oven mitts. She fleetingly wondered about tetanus—metal had scraped past skin—as she walked back inside. Under the stream of water from the kitchen faucet, flaps of skin on her knuckles moved like wet paper. The blood became a pale pink as it mixed with the water and flowed down the drain. As the sharp pain subsided and a dull throbbing took its place, she carefully put the skin back to where it had been before. Happy to see that no chunks were missing, she daubed her hands carefully with a towel, then went in search for some disinfectant and bandages. She knew untended simple infections could prove grave.

She was about to step back into the garage, realized how

tired she was, turned around, and sat down on her big, comfortable chair. She reached for her knitting needles, felt a twinge of pain from the tightness on the back of her hand, then stopped reaching. She reached for a magazine, then stopped. Her back fell against the chair. She sat and just thought.

After a long while of sitting, Shirley took out the magnifying glass she sometimes used for crossword puzzles and pulled out the newspaper article about the first annual pumpkin chucking contest. It had become frayed on the creases and the ink had smudged many of the words from her idly fingering it so often when it was in her pants pocket. She smoothed the paper out on the coffee table and looked at the photographs of the winning catapults. She studied them so hard and so close that what she stared at were no longer a parts of a machine, but individual dots of ink on newsprint. Unhelpful. She continued to rhythmically smooth out the piece of paper, letting the images lose focus, trying to visualize what she wanted to do as a whole. It didn't help, so she got up, walked into the garage, and push pinned the article onto the cork board above her workbench, next to the diagram of her work in progress.

Shirley sat down on her work stool and looked at the catapults in the newspaper. The pictures had cropped off the edges of the catapults, but she could see where their action came from, how the energy was supposed to transfer, the material that was used. This helped a bit, and Shirley's brain Rototilled and mulched that information. No final plan was immediately sprouting, but the barren feeling of hopelessness was being slowly replaced by the fertility of her thoughts.

She looked back up to the newspaper. It was the darndest thing. Even though she had looked at those pictures hundreds of times by then, a new detail could pop out of nowhere, plain as an ant on her counter top.

Shirley pulled the pin out of the cork board, brought the

paper up to her face, wrinkled her nose, and thought out loud. "Huh. It looks like a bicycle inner tube is keeping that throwing arm in place." She penciled a note into her plans.

She pictured her newest project, the entire catapult, from every little screw and bolt, to the garage door springs, to its stand. Her mind could zoom in on the microscopic details then whoosh back to see the contraption working as a whole.

A movement outside caught Shirley's gaze. She glanced through the window and the tree outside dipped and shuddered in the wind. She looked at the branches and leaves, all independent-ly moving, all connected to a trunk, fastened to the ground for over seventy-five years. The leaves: new, green, vulnerable, and shimmering. The trunk was wrinkled, knotted, and steady. It was the anchor, never going anywhere, but allowing the canopy of extending branches above her house to stretch out further and fur-ther. The tree, its trunk and branches, reminded Shirley of her granddaughter, Rachel, away at summer camp for a month, miss-ing her, but enjoying missing her. Enjoying the solitude, comfort-ed in the thought that it was finite and under good terms, and that Rachel would be back soon enough.

Tea—which Shirley had mistakenly purchased when she was looking at another brand and plopped it in her cart without know-ing—had a charging buffalo on its box. Lighting bolts shot from its nostrils in every direction. Holding true to the insinuation on the box, the tea had a lot of caffeine. And perhaps that's why Shirley felt a little jolt of courage, a simmering of "Let's get this started, ol' gal" after she cautiously sipped from her cup.

Mug of fresh tea in hand, Shirley stepped back into the garage. The leprous, dangerous medieval whats-a-ma-jig on her workbench was all she had been able to construct in the first two hours of work on her new experiment.

Inspiration hit like a single light bulb, activated by a string. It wasn't a Las Vegas billboard of buzzing and twisted neon with apoplectic flashes, screaming, "Inspiration! This Way! Do It Now!"

"Bolts, not screws," Shirley said to herself.

"Bolts, not screws," said to herself again, to drive the point home. "These little buggers need to stay in place."

Unable to make any real progress on removing the screws from the piece of angle iron she'd been dickering with, she put it aside.

Shirley had purchased three metal bed frames at separate garage sales, all for less than two dollars apiece. The frames, with the removal of just a couple of bolts, were collapsible. Shirley was trying to decide if she wanted her catapult collapsible, or not. She was keeping the option open.

She looked up at her schematic diagram that was push-pinned into corkboard in front of her. The funny thing with instructions is that good ones make more sense the longer they're studied. Like poetry and prayers, the more they're concentrated on, nuance and interior logic are revealed. Conversely, with bad instructions, although there's a diagram that looks whole, the more the parts are examined, the more obvious it becomes that the plan is merely a snapshot of failure or complete disintegration.

Shirley's diagram was meticulously penciled in on a big piece of paper, all to proper scale.

She started to work on part of the base of the catapult, which was little more than a long rectangle, eight feet long and two feet wide. It was a simple affair that only required the four pieces of metal be affixed at ninety-degree angles so the box would be true to evenly distribute the inevitable pressure of the catapult.

She was making a flat box.

First, Shirley mocked up how the pieces should fit together by snugging them near one another without affixing them. When everything was aligned, she made white grease pencil marks on the green-painted steel. She took one piece at a time and hammered into the metal with a center punch. It took two or three full strikes of the hammer on the punch to leave noticeable dimples in the metal.

Drill plugged into a power strip above the bench, proper size drill bit chucked tightly into the drill, a bead of oil placed in the center of the dimple, and Shirley was able to drill through the metal without much difficulty. It was definitely progress. After her first successful hole, she brought it up to the light for inspection. A small curlicue of shiny metal squiggled off the drill bit. Her smile quickly faded when Shirley looked down and saw a fresh new hole in the wood of her workbench.

"Aaahhh," Shirley muttered as she scavenged below the workbench and found a thick chunk of wood, which she then placed under the next piece of metal she planned on drilling.

The next five or six holes were drilled to plan. Shirley was getting the knack of it.

Shirley didn't see it, but on the opposite side of the metal she was about to drill was a knot of steel: a metal drip that had cooled and hardened into a bead.

Shirley, although attentive, had relaxed her grip on the piece she was drilling. She applied downward pressure, to pin the two-foot-long piece of metal to the workbench. The drill hummed in her right hand, bit into the metal, and began its twisting. She eased her grip when she realized she was about to get all the way through, and when she did, the tip of the drill bit snagged on that extra-tough metal gristle. It turned what the drill was stuck in into a propeller that, in quick succession, ripped itself out of Shirley's hand, smashed her mug of tea, came half circle, and walloped her in the ribs before she knew what was happening.

She let out a groan, but to her credit, didn't drop the drill, and just took her finger off the trigger. She stood stock-still to put together what had just happened. One of her favorite mugs that, up until moments before, had a print from a photograph of her parents screened on it, was in chunks. Tea was migrating towards her and flowing onto the floor. There wasn't much liquid. She'd almost finished the cup. The tea bag, which had been in the mug, was slapped against an adjacent wall, stuck there, dripping. It took several more seconds for Shirley to look at her right hand because she didn't want to move. She looked down at the drill and then she looked at the piece of metal that was stuck on perpendicularly at the end of the drill bit.

"Oh, glory be," Shirley said, as she put the incident together. She placed the drill back on the workbench, then felt her rib. The right side of her body wasn't faring well that day. She pushed on her ribs. They were sore. She took a deep, deliberate breath and held it. It didn't hurt any more by doing that, so it probably wasn't cracked, just bruised, maybe not even that.

Shirley tried to calm herself by sopping up the tea and collecting the biggest mug chunks, along with the curly metal shavings, into a rag. Her breathing had picked up. She was getting angry at herself again. Impatient. She took two steps away from her body.

The ghost of Shirley looked at Shirley-at-the-bench. Ghost Shirley surveyed the situation, and since she wasn't feeling aches and pains, began laughing at the teabag slapped onto the wall, at the geriatric hi-jinks, at the fact that Shirley-at-the-bench was really beginning to make a catapult out of bed parts. Ghost Shirley laughed and laughed and laughed until she merged back with Shirley-at-the-bench, who suddenly felt much better. Shirley tried to wiggle the metal free from the tip of the drill. She moved it back and forth, and it moved, but just a little bit. It was still firmly lodged.

Upon closer inspection, Shirley made another important discovery: a little lever that was just above the trigger. Shirley flipped it and the drill bit moved in the reverse direction. She pinned the piece back on the workbench, and within two seconds, the drill popped out. She'd bought the drill at a garage sale. There hadn't been an instruction manual. Otherwise, she would have read it twice before picking up the machine and would have known exactly how to reverse its action.

Shirley still had five more holes to drill. She placed the block of wood under the piece of metal so she wouldn't pock her workbench. She leaned heavily down on the metal and grasped it on both sides with one hand so it wouldn't whack her again like a karate chop. Activating the drill, it hummed against the metal, but made no progress. A quick whiff of befuddlement dissipated into an "Oh, yeah. Duh," as she flipped the lever from reverse and the bit began biting metal as it twirled.

It's amazing, Shirley thought to herself, that the simplest thing on paper: drill hole right here, had turned into a process with many definite, assumed, and hidden steps.

That day, there was only one more lesson Shirley could endure.

At first, she almost fainted, thinking that she was being splattered with a generous amount of her own blood. Over the din of the drill, she hadn't heard the can hit the floor and break open. Red paint grenaded out of it, covering everything from the concrete it impacted with, all the way up to Shirley's right side.

Shirley began to cry as the acrylic fumes filled her nostrils. She sobbed, even when she put the pieces together. The vibration of the drill had shaken the entire bench. Above the bench were paint cans. One of them had rattled off its shelf and cannon balled onto the floor below. She wasn't physically injured, but the indignity of being covered in cold, stinking red paint hurt. It was a different pain from what she felt in her knuckles and ribs, but it still stung.

She felt ashamed, blanketed by the dark side of discovery that people don't want to admit to. She felt literally covered in failure, as saturated and obvious as the paint that was beginning to burn and pinch her skin.

"How can I think of everything?" she asked herself out loud.

The paint didn't come off easily. She wasn't about to track

any of it inside and risk messing up the carpet or walls. Experiments and disorder were to take place in the garage. The house was to remain clean and orderly.

Shirley first focused on getting herself cleaned up. She found a beach towel, emptied out her car-washing bucket, filled it with warm water, and began sponging off her hand. Figuring that the liquid soaps for car washing were designed to remove road-borne tar and other gummy material, she squeezed healthy amounts of soap into the bucket, watched the bubbles rise, and began rubbing her body off with a sponge. The paint seemed to be swiping off, so Shirley removed her clothes, down to her underwear, and carefully placed the soiled items in a plastic bag.

Shirley made quick work of containing the spill. Rag after rag of paint was swiped off the workbench, the floor, and a gang load of jars that were splattered with it.

The water that flowed into the shop drain in the middle of the garage floor went from dark crimson to light carnation.

Convinced she'd gotten most of the paint off, she walked inside barefoot, and hopped in the shower. The hot water first felt like lead needles penetrating her skin. Then she warmed up. She continued to find hidden refuges of paint: inside her ear canal, tucked away behind a curl of hair, clumped on the tiny, fine hairs of her legs. So she continued scrubbing until she was convinced that she'd washed as much of the bad memory of the day away, paint along with it.

She toweled herself off, which took more time than usual since her right hand had begun to swell and her sore rib limited her range of motion. Opening the bathroom door and turning on the fan, she waited for the full-length mirror on the door to defog so she could perform a final inspection. She toed on some fuzzy slippers, which always felt good on her feet, like little hugs, then sat on top of the toilet seat, resting.

Standing up, she studied herself carefully, like a map of an old continent, which whispered that it had new details. Shirley was patient. She knew her life at this age was a marathon. How could it not be? There were very few situations that would make her want to hurry.

"Nope, no globs of paint," she said to her reflection. She smiled at herself. She liked her smile. She could have robbed banks with that smile. She took a step back to get a better look at Shirley-as-a-whole, not Shirley-piece-by-piece.

She removed her glasses, which had been thoroughly cleaned before she stepped into the shower. She cleaned them again out of reflexive habit, like she always did after taking a shower and having a lint-free towel handy. Then she compared her hands, side by side. The knuckles on her right hand were swollen and starting to bruise.

She looked at the mirror again, this time examining the two sides of her face.

"Dang, really?" Shirley said.

All of Shirley's body that had been exposed to the paint—the right side of her face, her forearm, the little ring where her pants didn't quite reach down to the top of her socks—was now pink. It was subtle, but Shirley felt like two-thirds of a carton of Neapolitan ice cream, which made her feel a little more obviously odd. It's one thing to feel a little bit crazy; in fact, it was probably normal. It's quite another for co-workers and neighbors to have some justification for arriving at the same conclusion.

After putting on clothes and re-wrapping her knuckles, her new pinkness wasn't half as obvious, since it wasn't in vivid contrast to the fields of her pale, white skin. Her face was slightly speckled, but the splotches were hidden by just a little foundation. Nothing drastic.

As Shirley put some milk on the stove for hot cocoa, she surveyed her day. She'd been able to drill fifteen holes in metal. That was in the good category. Four scraped knuckles, one rib that hurt, one damaged chunk of self-confidence, one work outfit out of commission, partially pink skin: those were in the bad category. But behind that all, tethered by a such a long string that she barely saw it when it was flickering at the back of her consciousness, was a new, small fire burning. A fire of creation was slowly burning inside of her and gaining in size.

As the milk began to steam and undulate from the heat, she poured it into a cup full of cocoa. She plopped a small handful of miniature marshmallows on top, and slowly watched them melt into the velvety brown liquid.

If only the catapult, Shirley thought, was as easy as making cocoa. She took a long sip. It steamed up her glasses as she walked towards her big, comfortable chair.

She spent the rest of the day recuperating, reading a book.

Sleep was a little troublesome. Any direct pressure on her ribs made her feel a tug or nudge of soreness near her chest. Luckily, she had no trouble sleeping on her back.

CHAPTER SIX
The X-Ray Eyes of Scientists

In the morning, after swabbing her knuckles with more anti-septic, she removed her nightshirt, expecting to see a large bruise over her rib. But nothing. Just pliable folds of skin. Cupping her hand, she gingerly probed her ribcage. There was no outward sign of damage. She squinted her eyes, which really didn't improve her vision, but made her feel like it did. She couldn't see anything different from the left side of her ribcage to the right side.

After putting on a blouse, she was in no hurry to get back into the garage. She was in no shape to continue building the cat-apult that day, but the idea that her workspace was still a mess irri-tated her sense of order. She tried to ignore its nagging, but that was like a tree ignoring a woodpecker hammering away at its trunk.

With her knuckles scraped and swollen, Shirley made anoth-er unsavory discovery, which put her in a funk: knitting was painful. Knitting and sleeping soundly were two of Shirley's favorite pastimes. She made some breakfast. Perhaps subcon-sciously pushing too hard for a small slice of redemption—even if it came solely as another cup of cocoa—she slurped too early. It scalded the roof of her mouth. The ridges of her palate flared from the heat because she was thinking of how to improve the catapult, not of blowing on hot liquid to make it cool. Such sim-ple things were biting her behind. Shirley's funk increased when she got a paper cut from opening a piece of mail, nevertheless she managed to put the makings of a stew into the crock pot to slowly simmer until suppertime. At least she'd have a meal.

Hands empty, head and back leaning softly against her chair, Shirley told herself, "Be still, ol' gal. Be still." She closed her eyes. At first, all she could hear was the rushing of blood behind her ears. As time when on and her breathing settled down, she began to hear the chirp and chatter of birds outside, the faraway hum of an airplane, the soft gusts of wind that rustled leaves and flexed branches. After all of those things had settled and calmed her, she mentally placed herself back at her workbench. She couldn't see nor remember all of the small details, she couldn't recall all of the exact equations and lengths and weights, nor did they seem to matter right then. The catapult was just the end result. She had to lasso the big picture first, rope it in, then tame it.

Can pumas be tamed? Shirley wondered.

Just as little kids vividly dream of some day becoming ballerinas and astronauts, cowboys and doctors, Shirley imagined herself as a scientist. A scientist who didn't make dumb mistakes, who wasn't a neophyte, who didn't get splattered with paint. A scientist with nerve, strong theories, and experiments which gave glistening, stainless results. The experiments would be unbreakable, like steel girders holding up a skyscraper of a new idea.

Shirley delved further into that scientist's brain and looked through that scientist's eyes. She realized something then: scientists have x-ray eyes. Well, the good scientists do. And not x-ray eyes to see people's underwear, and not just x-ray eyes to look inside of bones, by x-ray eyes into the world. Those x-rays can't penetrate everything but they provide more clues than normal sight. They bring out the contrast. They reveal, in the search for unity, hidden likeness. And when that scientist in Shirley's brain—which, by the way, looked essentially like Shirley but with a bleached white smock and fancier eye goggles—conducted an experiment, the veil between theory and practice was pulled away.

Shirley watched the scientist put a catapult together, piece by piece, load it up, and fire it. The motion entranced her: that sudden release from all that built up potential energy, the crackling whimper of springs, the snap of the tennis ball from its little cup into the steel gray sky. She played that part over and over again: the ball flying away from the catapult's arm. The satisfaction of accomplishment. Most impressive of all was that Shirley's scientist wasn't getting continually maimed. The scientist, although working hard, seemed invigorated. Shirley left the scientist, emboldened by her long string of successes, as she was hoisting a bowling ball onto the actuating arm of the catapult.

And then something dawned on Shirley, something that had been just below the surface of the water and was rising above, causing small ripples in her conscience, spreading light over everything like a sunrise. Learning how to drill a hole in a piece of metal was part of the experiment. Having a clean and orderly workspace was part of the experiment. Sitting down and thinking everything through before she lost a limb or blinded herself was part of the experiment. She knew if housecleaning, carpentry, first aid, and theory had all been summoned and were beginning to mix together, what she was aiming for couldn't be one irreducible fact, but a web of facts. It wasn't just a question of whether her physics were good or if the metal would bend and not break. It was all of that—everything she could fathom—and a little bit more. What she was looking for was a new sheet of knowledge, not just a stitch, not a single lightning bolt that would illuminate the right thing ultra-obviously and destroy everything else around it. Science wasn't like that. Science was a quilt that was being sewn before she was born and wouldn't ever stop being made. Shirley's experiment wasn't just a catapult. It was how to conjure up, from the intersection of all these different ideas raining all around her into a pure and simple device that would work as designed. Sure, hundreds of thousands of catapults had been built in the last five hundred years. This, however, was Shirley's first. It still remained a weapon of mathematics. And the Greeks and Romans didn't have modern, metal rollaway bed frames to work with.

By late morning, Shirley went back out to the garage. Using her not-so-good, outside mop, she cleaned the floor once more. The thinned-out paint had started to congeal; it looked and acted more and more like blood. To a careful eye, the crime scene had all the appearances of a spontaneous and messy birth.

Favoring her left hand, Shirley scrubbed and scrubbed: jars of nuts and bolts, little metal suitcases for socket sets, cardboard boxes that housed power tools and kept them dust free. She let be the spread-out constellation of speckles on the ceiling. They were far out of her reach. Besides, she rationalized to herself, when was the last time she had ever looked at her garage's ceiling?

She went back on the offensive and filled a bucket with bleach and water. By the third mop-over, the concrete floor was as clean as the day it was poured. The red pigment swirled in the bucket. It looked as if it contained a bleeding hunk of just-cut beef.

Shirley grabbed a short stepladder, opened it up, and wiggled it to make sure it was secure. As she reached upward, a twinge of pain visited her. Her rib was neither in excruciating pain nor was it completely fine.

It's amazing, Shirley thought, how all the parts of the body are connected.

One by one, she removed the cans of paint from above the workbench, inspecting them for red dots while wiping them free of dust.

Satisfied that the area was clean, Shirley took the rest of the day off, with the exception of adding carrots and celery to the stew two hours before it would be ready. She ate, put all the leftovers in little, sealable plastic boxes, and cleaned her dishes. She was pleased that her knuckles had begun to scab over. She couldn't do anything more about her rib, although it very well may have been cracked after all.

Perhaps it was the visitation of slight, nagging pain along with the reassuring, subtle feeling of the body repairing itself, but for whatever reason, that night Shirley's dreams were vivid and full of ancient warriors. Engines of war roared in her sleep. Hundreds of men loaded rocks as big as her entire house onto siege craft as tall as any building in her hometown. Throwing arms creaked as loudly as if all the trees in a forest were being bent at once. The machines bucked and lashed wildly as projectiles were released. Her point of view was that of a bird's, flying over a medieval castle. Gigantic rocks flew up and over the castle's walls. Intermittently, smaller, oval objects were launched from the smaller catapults. Landing, they didn't register percussive hits that dislodged stone, but splatted, oozed honey, and released thousands of angry bees seeking vengeance for their destroyed hives. Villagers shrieked as they were swarmed.

It was a long dream, a dream that made Shirley partially ashamed at the lack of the "civil" part of civilization. Bird Shirley, high above on a column of warm air, coasting on widespread wings, saw a flying horse that had no wings. And since this was a dream, Bird Shirley swooped down, next to the horse which smelled of death, its tongue a gray, expressionless piece of meat lolling out of its mouth, its body invisibly overflowing with some horrible virus or bacteria. It cleared the top of the castle. The horse landed in a sad symphony of broken bones, escaping intestines, and explosive mucilage. The barbarians were catapulting dead horses.

Shrieks filled the air. Human beings moved like disease. The peasants, who, through the unlucky roulette of conception, timing, and geography, were beholden to the men in shining metal and held-aloft swords, were those she felt the most for.

The siege continued. Casks of hot tar and burning oil found their targets and the smell of burning human flesh added a charred dimension to the pall. Bird Shirley was wishing that the dream would end, but no matter which way she would try to fly away, she couldn't get away from the battle. A human scream came louder and louder, higher and higher. They were now catapulting people. Hundreds of yards into the atmosphere, humans flew in awkward spasms, clutching at the air, hoping to grasp onto the rungs of an invisible ladder. Bird Shirley turned around just in time, cawed loudly, and was swallowed into the belly of a screaming woman as she began her descent to the earth below.

Shirley bolted upright in her bed, quickly realized that she herself hadn't been launched from a medieval catapult as a spy or a traitor, and began to rethink some assumptions.

"Why am I making a catapult?" she asked herself, her room dark with the exception of the dim illumination from the dial of her bedside clock. "I don't want to hurt anyone. I don't want to take over a city. I don't even want to impose my will on anybody." Her head spun.

And then she remembered. A whisper came from the center of her brain. Science. Science and math. Creation. Just because some greedy, land-hungry people who feared anybody who didn't think like them had hired engineers to build engines to break down castle walls didn't mean that the science was awful and vindictive. How science was used and why it was used; those were the keys. Science was science, just like nature is nature. Shirley just wanted to launch a couple of tennis balls from what used to be a bed frame and move up from there. No killing of the innocents. No biological warfare. No dead, flying horses. No launched human beings. Just tennis balls and a way to feel like she was putting a dent in her world by launching projectiles back against all the days she'd given to work solely for other people's gain.

It took her a while to fall back asleep. When sleep came, it was a dark, quiet cloak.

Shirley decided that she needed a week for her body to repair. She also felt that her brain was overheating, so she went to the library after work and picked up a couple of books that were as light, fun, and filling as cotton candy.

CHAPTER SEVEN
It Looked Like an Adult Erector Set

"Rachel, you're a good kid," Shirley said to the postcard in her hand, reading a short note from her granddaughter as she walked back from her mailbox and in through her front door. Although the horticultural summer camp was only two hours away, they both missed one another. They'd made a promise to not make contact by phone unless there was an emergency.

Rachel had enjoyed the soft clicking sounds of her heels on the pavement as she had walked to the bus station by herself, bag on her back, and relished the fact that she did it on her own. It was only a five-mile walk, but the feeling of independence, of not being the crying girl who literally clawed her mother's shirt like an opossum when dropped off at camp, made her feel wiser, emotionally older, more confident. Rachel didn't need anyone to drop her off or pick her up. She was her own woman. Being an orphan, Rachel knew the difference between a month away from the woman she loved the most—Grandma Shirley—and death. A month was easy.

Rachel had earned a counselor-in-training scholarship to the month-long camp, a result of winning the science fair in her high school two years in a row. Her experiments had all dealt with plants. Rachel was a budding geneticist. Her teachers had first suspected an over-helpful parent, funneling their unfulfilled academic fantasies through their child, a practice most often reserved for fathers pressuring their sons in football and wrestling.

The soft murmurs of disbelief began when Rachel was a freshman, yet the inquisition withered on the vine each and every time she was asked to explain the experiments in fine detail. The judges, whose eyes at the beginning of the inquiry would stab at her with exposed knife points of disbelief, would soften, fold away their blades, and eventually end up glassy. The kid bored them, no doubt, but she apparently knew what she was talking about. She also intimidated the judges with theories they'd skimmed over at the back of their own science books that their classes never got to by the end of the year. Hell, they'd thought, if I don't have to teach it, I don't have to read it.

Rachel had undoubtedly eclipsed the league of Styrofoam-on-a-stick solar system models and baking soda-belching plaster of Paris volcanoes she was up against. And no one could deny, that at age twelve, she'd grown the biggest goddamn crooked neck squash they'd ever seen. It had to be carted in on a wagon. Each of the judges idly thumped it. The thing was real. The kid wasn't pulling a hoax and she said she was developing ways it wouldn't rot so fast after it'd been picked, that she was working on how it could become naturally pest-resistant. They had to give her first place.

When asked how she'd come up with her ideas, her answer was succinct.

"I read a lot. I've also got a garden." Rachel had picked up her grandmother's gift of understatement.

And when asked how she found the books she was looking for, her answer was just as abrupt.

"The library. I get them through inter-library loan. I'm also making friends in the horticulture community. We share ideas."

Rachel always brought along her notes and research, in a big manila accordion file. They never asked her to open it up, to slip off the big elastic band that captured all that information, and back up her data.

Rachel proudly thumped her elephantine squash.

The judges tacked a big, blue ribbon to a panel on the poster board's display.

Rachel's specialty of specialties was pumpkins, from real tricky genetic things like plasmodesmata to how to control their shapes.

So, at the bottom of every post card she wrote to Grandma Shirley once a week, there was a hand-drawn pumpkin with a big, toothy smile.

Shirley always wrote back promptly. She felt like she was telling gray lies, like, "I've been working on a new experiment. Nothing fancy. A small machine. Velocities and trajectories." Shirley didn't lie, so her thoughts weren't blackened, but she knew her stories were incomplete. Gray. She didn't write of her feelings of humiliation and embarrassment of not being able to turn a screw. Of being slightly maimed. Of the experiment punishing her, of it not working, and her scraped knuckles. But she didn't want Rachel to worry or to feel bad. She wanted Rachel to have fun and be protected from the gristle and grime that always accumulates in life, like dirt on a fan or splattered grease on a stovetop. Rachel had been through enough. Being born without a mother and father was more than enough pain for anyone to start out with.

With fresh eyes, a fully flexible right hand, and a ribcage that barely nagged her, Shirley finally got down to serious business. Securing one end of a piece of metal to a vice, which was bolted securely to her workbench, she made quick work of drilling all the holes. The simplest measures prevented her from being whacked by flying debris. On the floor of the garage, she placed all of the parts beside one another, just to make sure she hadn't messed up on a decimal point or marked a wrong end. With the frame looking like something that had just been surprised in a cartoon, all a little bit stretched out, Shirley was convinced that it could reasonably be snugged together. Ratchet in hand, she tightened nylon-capped nuts onto hardened steel bolts through the holes in the metal. Shirley enjoyed the simple sounds of the clicking ratchet, the pleasing ninety-degree angles of two pieces of metal butting up against one another, the reassuring, immutable feeling of something slowly coming together the way it was planned without it whacking her. Within two hours, the bottom of the catapult was finished. It was time to start working on the vertical elements.

Shirley's design called for four garage door springs. The idea was that, unloaded, the business end of the throwing arm would be a little over her head. Almost at the very tip of the throwing arm would be a cup. In there, she'd place a tennis ball. Then, with a boat winch secured to the base with four bolts, she would thread a fine chain around the throwing arm. She would ratchet the arm all the way to the ground while the garage door springs expanded, putting a good six feet of tension on them. Shirley, not completely happy with this setup, and thinking that she would improve on this bit after a couple test runs, would release the chain by whacking it off the end of the throwing arm with a broom handle. That was the plan.

Methodically, she began bolting together the upright supports. They were little more than two rectangular frames. One would be bolted at ninety degrees from the base. On top of it, a reinforced, round pole would serve as the surface that the throwing arm would pivot upon. On the bottom of the rectangle of the support were hooked pegs that the garage door springs were fastened to. The third rectangle of metal was simply a way of supporting the whole contraption so it wouldn't bend in half. It created a triangle of space between the base and pivot point on top, which Shirley positioned herself inside of as she secured more bolts.

Truth be told, it looked like an adult Erector set: skeletal but functional. Shirley had yet to install the springs or make the throwing arm. She rocked the frame back and forth, side to side. It wiggled a lot, much more than she cared for. She walked around the inert about-to-be machine with a critical eye, hoping that it would whisper a remedy. She stood on top of her work stool, looking down on the catapult-in-making. She lay on the concrete on her belly and looked at it at an ant's level, straight on. Before the words formed pictures in her brain, from the side of the house, she found a ten-foot-long piece of wood that was about two feet wide and a little over an inch tall. It slid snugly into the front of the base. It looked like a long, flat tongue depressor. Properly screwed beneath the catapult, it provided all the front and back stability she could hope for.

With visions of tennis balls flying, Shirley whispered, "This is definitely progress."

She knew the throwing arm would work better if it was a specialized metal. It had to be strong enough to withstand all of the tension, yet light enough so it would get the maximum amount of whip powered by the garage door springs.

She tested one of the pieces of metal she was thinking about using for the throwing arm. Clamping one end of it in her vice, she put all her weight against it, and it bent far too easily. Shirley scavenged around her house but couldn't find anything that struck her as workable throwing arm. It wasn't a thankless scavenge. She took the stabilizing arms off of an old house trailer. A series of holes drilled, some ratchet action, and an hour later, the side-to-side wiggling of the catapult had been reduced to almost nothing. The catapult was now firmly planted. The possibility of it being collapsible and highly portable had faded away.

Shirley glanced outside, was surprised that it was dark, realized that she'd been working for ten hours already, was in desperate need of some soup, and called it a day. Her body was definitely on the mend.

CHAPTER EIGHT
The Antlers of a Jackalope,
Shotgunned Beers, and a Stop Sign

All day at work Monday, although her memos were up to snuff and her reports were filed on time, Shirley couldn't stop thinking about the throwing arm. She needed something durable. She thought about it so much through lunch that she stopped half way through her bag of potato chips and only ate half of her tuna fish sandwich. Using a paper clip to seal the top of the potato chip bag and wrapping up the unfinished sandwich on the way back to her office, she wished the fluorescent lights that she passed under could shoot a good idea directly into her brain. By the time she got to her desk, nothing new had flashed inside of her mind, nor did it for the remaining four hours of her workday. She continued to type at a respectable sixty words-per-minute.

As she was driving home, a man in a 4x4 truck, which looked like every conceivable metal part of it was injected with steroids, cut her off and pulled in front of her at a stop sign. From his trailer hitch dangled a wide, dirty white sock with what looked like two balled-up socks inside of it. As the man punched the gas and sprayed arcs of gravel, Shirley got it.

"Oh, those are his truck's testicles," she said matter-of-factly.

Surprisingly, Shirley caught up to the man at the next stop sign. He appeared to be finishing a drum solo on his steering wheel, then went into an extended guitar solo, while his head jerked back and forth. Shirley knew better than to honk. She just sat fifty feet behind him and waited. No need for antagonism. Sometimes folks just need a little space to clear their heads out. In no time, he punched the gas and took off fast.

Perhaps empowered by the guitarist's blistering fretwork coming from his car stereo, perhaps made happier by the fourth tallboy that day, shotgunned by the way of the antler of the jackalope hot-glued onto his dashboard he used to puncture his beer cans, or perhaps as a result of being laid off two hours prior—the mystery may never be solved—the man in the truck apparently had his fill of stop signs for the day. It was also obvious to Shirley that the man had done many times what he was about to do. She recognized expertise.

The truck lunged forward, hit the post, and snapped the stop sign in two. The truck's gigantic push bar made a clean break in the pole.

The stop sign became lodged under the truck, fanning a bewilderingly long arc of sparks behind it.

The man let out at long "Yaahooooo!" and pumped his fist out the window.

He was a pro. Before the next stop sign, he spotted a small berm on the right side of the road, fishtailed onto the dirt, launched his truck, and smacked the sign in mid-air, about five feet off the ground. His left hand formed a fist, which he stuck out of the window while in flight. The sign bent and flew away, discarded like a soggy paper lollipop stick.

In her rearview mirror, Shirley saw the flashing lights of the police, and pulled over to the side of the road.

The police car sped past Shirley, its motor roaring, the wind it created shaking her car as it passed. The man in the truck, in a further testament to his driving ability and to show that he had more than merely two methods of wiping out rural traffic signs, yanked hard on his steering wheel when the police car was about to be upon him, spinning his truck ninety degrees. The rear quarter panel of his truck snapped another stop sign, right at the base. A perfect, clean break.

The man put his truck in low four, gunned it, and broke off right through a field, the police car in tow. The last she saw of the man was of him throwing a freshly empty beer can into the bed of his truck.

At least he doesn't litter, Shirley thought.

Shirley hadn't seen that much excitement in years. As she stopped at the intersection where the last stop sign should have been standing, she looked over at it in the dirt on the far side of the street. She drove up to it. It wasn't bent in the slightest. It looked like had just been unbolted and laid down.

A chain reaction of mental light bulbs finally sizzled to life.

Stop sign. Durable steel. Throwing arm. One of two cops in the immediate vicinity busy. I have room in the station wagon. She glanced around, conspiratorially. No traffic. Palms sweating, she fumbled with the keys to open up the rear door of the station wagon. Then she ran-walked to the sign, bent at the knees, and lifted with her back. She didn't want to leave any drag marks. She placed it pole-end first into the wagon. It barely fit. She covered the sign with a blanket, then—as always—obeyed all of the traffic laws in the state of Delaware the rest of the way home. Harry S. Truman had been President of the United States the last time Shirley had stolen something, and although she frowned on the practice, she couldn't help but feel a special, tingling thrill.

She waited until nightfall to take the stop sign out of the station wagon and snuck it into the garage.

Tuesday came and Shirley found out how hard it is to take a public sign off of its post. The powers that be had sneakily made the bolt heads so they were easy to affix but impossible to remove with a screwdriver, so Shirley cut the heads off with an electric grinder.

Returning from work on Wednesday, again checking the four corners for approaching traffic, Shirley dropped the de-poled stop sign back off at its intersection. She had no use for the sign and, as an assiduous taxpayer, was feeling a small measure of guilt.

By Friday, her rib had stopped hurting altogether and on Friday evening, she was back in the garage. The pole looked great. It had a little flex—Shirley supposed it was so it didn't break in high winds—for a nice whipping effect, but the metal didn't seem stressed and always returned to its original shape, even if she put all of her weight against it when it was clamped into the vice.

She placed the pole in a mock-up. The high end of the pole rested on the top of the catapult, where the top of the garage door springs would be attached. The other end was currently on the ground.

Shirley measured twice and made her markings with a white grease pencil. She removed the pole and began drilling a series of holes. The stop sign pole took drilling well. She slid the gooseneck of a mountain bike's handlebars into the end of the pole. The handlebars extended from the end of the pole in a "T." She then drilled a hole through the pole and the gooseneck of the handlebars and bolted them together. Her plan was to affix the top ends of the garage door springs onto the handlebars. The rubber grips on the handlebars provided extra hold, so the springs wouldn't just zing off when they slackened.

About a foot from the tip of the pole that was lying on the floor, Shirley drilled a hole through both an old gelatin mold and the pole, and fastened them together. The gelatin mold would serve as a cup to put the tennis ball in.

Shirley began to tire. She didn't want to overwork herself. She had the entire weekend ahead of her.

CHAPTER NINE
Junkyards and Resurrection

After a breakfast of oatmeal and orange juice, Shirley clapped her hands together, mentally surveyed what she had to do, and got to it.

The springs felt like heavy, dead black snakes and made sharp, eerie sounds as she wrestled with them. They wiggled in her hands before they were positioned, loaded, and stretched. Like a catapult in the newspaper article, the higher end of the throwing arm was lashed perpendicularly onto the elevated support arm with lengths of rubber bicycle inner tubes tied with strong knots. Shirley designed it so that when a tennis ball was discharged, the arm wouldn't just fly along with it. She'd read that the ancient Romans had used pig's grease to lubricate the friction between those two spots, so she used some solid vegetable shortening.

It was almost finished. All that was left was to hook a cable to the end of the arm, winch it down, load in a tennis ball, and let it fly.

Not wanting to rip a hole in her garage's ceiling, she huffed and puffed, and slowly wiggled, inched, screeped, and scraped the catapult out of the garage. It took well over half an hour and Shirley was pooped by the time it was fully in the driveway.

But first, Shirley wanted to see some action.

She threaded the cable over the end of the arm and began

winching it down. She put on her helmet. Ratchets engaged cogs. Shirley took her time. Catapults work by storing tension—the same as crossbows—but on a larger scale. The winch allowed Shirley to put a great deal of energy into the catapult over a period of time. Then all of that energy would be released at once. The catapult made some settling sounds, and the springs creaked, but it all looked good. When the arm touched the ground, Shirley locked the winch.

She located her broom handle and, from the side, gave the cable a tentative, but solid hit. It didn't budge. She tried whacking it a couple more times. No progress. She wound up, full force, let out a barely audible yelp as she swung, and that did the trick.

The catapult's arm shot forward in a blur, and the entire catapult jolted and shuddered like a just-roped steer. The power impressed Shirley, but she was worried about the firing mechanism. It was too messy and too dangerous, like a chainsaw without a guard and bad wiring.

Shirley padded inside, poured herself another glass of orange juice, and came to the conclusion that hitting the chain off the end of a pole loaded with tension was just sloppy and hazardous. It was no solution. A real thinker, Shirley surmised, doesn't master their experiments through force, but by understanding.

Shirley walked outside, backed away from the catapult, and leaned against the hood of her car. Gently, she placed her glass of orange juice on the hood. She stared at the catapult, wanting it to grow lips and start talking to her like a patient does to a psychologist. Tell her what it wanted to be fixed.

Knowing she was being silly and very far from the serious scientist she was shooting for, she picked up her glass and wiped off the ring of water it'd left on the car's hood. She looked down. Under the metal, on the other side of where her palm rested, came her answer. It was as if her hand had an eye in it. A kind of x-ray.

"Holy right!" Shirley squealed.

She found the latch by hand. She didn't have to see it with her eyes.

She popped the hood. It was an older car, one that didn't have a cable that had to be activated from inside to release the hood. "Yes! That'll do it," she said to herself as she looked at the very simple mechanism. Her mind was in a sprint.

"Bolt a little loop at the end of the throwing arm. Winch it down, have it click into the latch"—a latch exactly like the one that kept her car's hood from flying off when she drove down the street—"and release it with a lever. No more hitting things with sticks, old gal. You're not a barbarian."

Shirley was so excited that she was half way up her driveway before she remembered she had forgotten her wallet. Almost trembling, she audibly slowed herself down.

"It's okay," Shirley said to herself. "Think. Where are you going? Junkyard. What are you getting? A hood latch off a very large vehicle. A semi. A dump truck. Something like that. What do you need to remove the parts with?" She made a travelling tool bag of wrenches, screwdrivers, and sockets. She completed her mental checklist, down to some extra money for a snack if the hunt proved to be long.

As she drove to the junkyard, she kept removing her foot from the accelerator. "Slow down," she reminded herself. "Marathon."

A man about Shirley's age looked up from a newspaper as she approached the entrance in bright orange galoshes, toting a tool bag. His hands were stained almost black with oil, burned and scarred with decades' worth of handling hot and stubborn metal. His forearms were filthy, as were his clothes. He was a man, content in his natural environment, unashamed. On a quick glance, it wasn't clear where his arms ended and the sleeves of his rolled-up shirt began.

Shirley waited patiently for the man to lower his paper.

"What you in the market for today?" the old man asked, deferentially.

"Industrial-grade hood latch, sir."

"That it?" The man was used to people leading up to an impossible part request or trying out a dance of part numbers to impress him.

Shirley nodded.

"No specific make?"

Shirley shook her head.

"No specific model?"

Shirley shook her head.

"No specific year?"

"I just want the strongest one you've got," Shirley offered. "I'm going to be using it for something different than latching a hood. It has to be very strong. The strongest."

"You're in luck," the man said as he gently folded the newspaper and neatly placed it on his desk. "Follow me." He was so dark with grime that when he walked outside, under the gray sky, it looked like he was cast in a shadow.

"I can find it," Shirley replied. "Just tell me where it is. No need to bother."

"Follow me," the man said again. His voice was warm, his face placid. "Nothing happening today. Nobody's come in. Wanted to walk around the yard anyways. Got an excuse now." He walked steadily, like a man walking through a field where the location of explosive mines had been memorized. His legs kept exact measurements.

As Shirley followed the sure-footed man through the stacked rows of cars, she couldn't help but think of cemeteries. Machines that are dead are above ground, in a manner that each and every useful part of them can eventually be picked off, piece by piece, to help another machine from ending up next to them. Humans' bodies are buried or burned when they die. Human parts simply decay.

Shirley didn't become depressed because she thought beyond human bodies and into human minds. The really good ideas are like well-ordered junkyards. Small ideas, or ideas that didn't seem that important at one time—or couldn't be proven when they first were born—could be easily found and stripped from larger theories that had been driven into the ground or wrecked. All these ideas could be carefully removed then made to work anew. Junkyard reincarnation.

"Sir, you've got the most orderly junkyard I've ever seen," Shirley said to the man's back as they approached the truck he was absolutely positive had the toughest hood latch in the yard.

"Makes everything easier to find. Most people don't notice anything except the prices and the dog shit." Without looking, he reached under the hood of a hulking, blunt-nosed machine and popped the hood. The truck's radiator grill looked like a gigantic, sullen mouth. "Something like this what you're looking for?" The man backed away and Shirley looked inside the truck's maw.

The blade of the hood's release mechanism was about a foot long. The latch was heavy steel. The action was fluid when Shirley clicked the hood down, then released it with the lever. She did this three times, just to be sure.

"That looks perfect," Shirley observed. "It feels strong."

"You want all the bits?" the man asked. "The hardware?"

"That'd be great. Please."

Out from pockets in his pants and jacket that Shirley hadn't seen, the man produced two adjustable wrenches and began unfastening the parts before she could interject or protest. She was fully prepared to pull her own parts. The man made short work of the removal and gently handed each part to Shirley when he was done. Whipping out a soiled shop rag from his back pocket, he cupped all of the bolts and washers into it, tied it off at the top, and handed the bundle over to Shirley.

"Studebaker," the man said. "Built to not wear out. Bolted, not welded, so it could be replaced without damaging the hood or using a torch. Old like me." The man hadn't broken a sweat. His muscles barely strained, their memories full of hard labor. For the man, the motions were as easy and sure as an accountant ticking away at a keyboard.

"That it?" the man asked. "Sure you don't need nothing more?"

"That's it. These are the last pieces I need."

"All right."

The man lead Shirley back through the ordered maze along a different path than which they'd come and ended up going through the back door of his office.

"What're you going to use the latch for?" he asked while looking for a receipt pad.

"A catapult," Shirley answered.

"Sounds like a lot of fun." He smiled slightly. His teeth were mottled but were much whiter than his surrounding face. His face lit up. He looked like an odd professor. The tone of his voice changed considerably. "This world," he extended one hand out, palm up, and fanned far beyond his junkyard, "is powered by science. This, here," he pointed to the ground and made a circular motion with his index finger, "is not a graveyard. For any person to abandon an interest in machines—even in a place that many see as full of ruins, as a place for vultures with toolboxes—is to walk with open eyes towards slavery. Too many think in absolutes. Of life *or* death. There is life in death. Death in life. I hope the parts work, and here is your receipt." His eyebrows were as thick and animated as furry caterpillars, which arced on his forehead when he asked, "What are you going to catapult?"

"Tennis balls."

"What're you using for tension?"

"Four garage door springs."

"Those'll hold just fine," he said, nodding to the pieces of metal in Shirley's hands. "Although I don't think hood latches are pressure rated." He wrinkled his brow slightly. "Seven bucks."

"I have to pay you for your labor," Shirley reminded him.

"Already figured that in."

Shirley pulled out the money, exact, knowing she was being undercharged.

"Be careful," the old man said.

"Pardon?" Shirley asked as she placed the latch in her tool bag. The sound of metal-on-metal dulled his words.

"Be careful." He smiled again. "Devils come out. Don't ignore the details. Stored energy devices need to be handled with caution, constant tending, and care."

"Thanks. I'm trying to be."

Shirley smiled back as the man sat down, unfolding what he had previously been reading. "Come back if you need anything else," he said from the other side of the paper.

CHAPTER TEN
The Measurements of Slaughter

When Shirley got home, she popped the hood on her station wagon and studied how the latch worked. How it released. How it was fastened. Catch, release. She pulled up on the hood of her car with the catch in place. Shirley wasn't very strong, but the catch didn't budge. Catch, release. So simple and effective. Solely seeing something working as it was designed to and then making it work yourself often proves to be a challenge. Shirley knew that. She drew a diagram and placed it on the ground, in front of the catapult.

With the throwing arm slack, she removed the garage door springs. With the arm touching the ground, there would be no question on how everything would match up.

Spooling out an electrical cord, she plugged the drill in, carefully measured, made holes, and tightly fastened the bolts into place. Within an hour, the hood latch on the catapult was working as advertised. Catch, release. She reattached the garage door springs to the throwing arm, winched it down, and clicked it into place. The latch held. Shirley winced as she placed her palm on the release latch. It was stiff and full of tension. She flinched as she began applying tension to the release latch. It didn't budge. The good news was that the latch continued to withstand the pressure. It was holding true. No creaking. No give.

Shirley knew an old trick and went in search of a pipe. After several that were too small, she found one that fit snuggly over the latch lever. The length of the pipe gave her an extra three feet of leverage. She barely leaned on it and the catapult released the throwing arm. It bucked like a wild bull, resisting being tamed, its genitalia being yanked by a rope.

Shirley was in business. She could taste it.

She loaded up a tennis ball, cranked the winch, hit the release lever, and off the tennis ball went, out of sight, in a fluorescent green arc.

Shirley tried to act cool and inconspicuous as she scoured the neighborhood for the ball, hoping that it hadn't gone through someone's window, dented a car hood, or come down on a napping cat.

After half an hour, she gave up her search and returned home. It was starting to get dark. Another light bulb flashed above her.

"Hey," she said to herself in a way that was particular to making a discovery, which was almost always accompanied by the snap of her fingers. "What about attaching a string to the tennis ball? That way I'll only have to use one ball."

Rather than lug the catapult back inside—since she'd be using it the next day—she covered it with a tarp, which cloaked its details. This made the contraption more conspicuous, labeling it as something to hide: contraband.

In the morning, after a bowl of saltines crushed up into milk, Shirley had a tennis ball securely squeezed into a vice. With an ice pick, she poked a hole through the tennis ball and wiggling the pick around, so the hole would remain. Next, she threaded a knitting needle with some yarn, forced it through the hole in the tennis ball, and tied it off.

Shirley knew that the yarn wouldn't last very long. She also knew that it would give the ball a tremendous amount of drag, but she knew she had 300 yards of yarn in a new spool and that it was brightly colored: an electric fuchsia. It would be easy to see in flight, like a tracer round out of a rifle. She tested the knot at the end by letting the ball slide out of her hand and swung it around and around over her head in a ten-foot circle. She looked like a very brightly colored cowgirl with a neon lasso.

Tarp pulled off, she tied the other end of the yarn to the catapult's throwing arm, right below the cup where the ball and the rest of the yarn would rest until launched. Everything seemed up to snuff as she began winching the arm back and clicking it into the locked position. She leaned against the release lever and the arm leapt skyward. The ball shot out, once again in an arc, but this time much more shallowly. The gray sky had a thin purple line through it for several seconds as the yarn lazed back to earth, fluttering through invisible air currents. The yarn hadn't become taut.

Shirley hopped on her bike. The tennis ball was easy to find. It was in the middle of the road, surrounded by loops of purple. Shirley guesstimated that there were at least one hundred more yards of yarn before the ball tested the limits of its tether. This disappointed Shirley. She thought the catapult would be stronger as she removed the end of a broom handle from her back pocket and began respooling the yarn onto it. The activity reminded her of days filled with flying kites. The bundle of yarn got bigger. It was filled with twigs, bits of leaves, and small rocks that Shirley didn't remove.

"Adding more springs isn't the answer," she said to herself. "There's plenty of tension."

She fell to silence as she walked down her driveway and stared. "I don't want to make you bigger. Not now," she told the catapult.

She studied the catapult like a patriot studies a flag while pledging allegiance to it or how an alcoholic studies her last bottle when it's almost empty.

Shirley felt small, biblically small. Like she was battling a giant.

And then it hit her, as solid as if a rock had been thrown at her head. "A sling. Barely appreciable increase in weight. Attach it to the end of the arm. Put the ball inside the sling. Get an extra couple of feet of swing to sweep through the air before it releases. It should work."

Electrified by the easy opportunity to increase the firepower with a minimal amount of extra effort, Shirley made quick work of adding a loop of rope and fashioning a little harness out of a leather belt for the tennis ball and yarn.

Half an hour later, she was back at the catapult.

Taking the junkyard man's advice, she tested the nuts and bolts of the slack catapult with a wrench. None of them had loosened, so Shirley began winching the throwing arm down until it clicked into place.

Giddy, Shirley absent-mindedly tossed aside the wrench as she reached for her helmet, not quite ready to fire the catapult, but getting into position. She could have put the wrench in her back pocket. She could have walked over to her tool bag and dropped in inside. But she didn't. She was standing directly behind the catapult—three feet behind it, at the backward reach of the new sling, she was to discover—when it happened. The wrench she had thrown aside hit the lever; not hard, but barely. Enough to trigger the catapult into action.

A blur of bright green and fuchsia flashed before Shirley as the sling whipped out from behind the catapult and stuck her on its upswing. The tennis ball rocketed from its harness and was still in an upward trajectory when the yarn became taut and snapped free from the catapult. Escaping, it was a green comet with a purple tail.

Shirley, unfortunately, didn't see this progress, and was understandably concerned with the blood that was leaping from her face and a very weird pain her brain didn't quite know how to process. No bones felt touched, just skin and flesh. She leaned forward to avoid getting blood on her clothes. As she did, she stared down at her sweater, which was sliced open in a straight line, like a hog opened up with a knife. She touched her throat. Blood transferred to her fingertips. She did the same with her lips. More blood. The bottom of her chin. The bottom of her nose. She cupped her hand over her mouth, scared to breathe deeply, fearing that vital organs might spill out. A thin red line of blood was the report as she pulled her hand into view. She didn't want to move. Her glasses, amazingly, were still in place on her face.

She felt sick. Sick from not understanding what has just happened. Sick from seeing her own blood pulse out of her body to the rhythm of her accelerated heartbeat. Sick from the hurt she knew she was probably going to feel once the adrenaline wore off. Sick from failure to recognize tripwires into disaster.

She felt silly and vulnerable and crazy. She began talking to herself.

"What am I doing? Getting myself killed? For what? What's wrong with knitting?" The catapult seemed momentarily silly. "You're too old to die like this."

She still didn't know what had happened, how she'd been bloodied. Fear mixed with pain and she began to cry.

Fortunately, the scratches weren't deep, just quick to bleed. She looked down at her stomach and pulled up her blouse. There wasn't even the slightest scratch on her belly. Not a mark. Her sweater had taken the brunt of the blow.

Seeing that she wasn't bleeding as profusely as she first thought, and that blood wasn't dripping between her fingers as she cupped her mouth, she walked into the house, ending up in the bathroom. When she removed her hand from her face, what startled her wasn't solely the long scratch that started at the bottom of her chin and ended at the top of her forehead, but how utterly straight it was. She removed her glasses. There was the tiniest nick in the frames, right in the middle of the bridge, where they rested on her nose. She felt like she was subconsciously measuring herself for a highly calculated slaughter, like old recipe books that explained where to cut for each piece of meat available from a cow. This unnerved Shirley greatly. She cried some more.

Her sweater—it was a work sweater and a little dirty and a little thin—needed more care than her skin, which was responding well to a small application of antiseptic and some antibiotic cream to stave off possible infection. She would have to call in sick until the mark healed. It was too obvious. A week, maybe less, she figured. The line was fingernail-scratch deep. Just enough to draw blood.

Shaky, with more confidence bled from her than actual blood, she walked back outside to face the perpetrator. The catapult stood there, silent, a machine at rest. Shirley walked up to the dangling sling, reached up, and put two fingers up to it. A small bead of blood transferred to her fingertips from a tiny burr. A piece of metal was stuck in the rope. Merely a metal shaving with a sharp edge. It was firmly imbedded, Shirley found out, as she tried to tug it free. It wouldn't budge.

Shirley felt protected by angels' wings, yet scraped by the devil's toenail.

Something so small, so inconsequential. It could have killed her, blinded her, or gored her if it was just a little bit longer or if she had been standing a little bit closer. She quit picking at the piece of metal, leaving it there as a small reminder to be mindful of the catapult at all times, loaded or unloaded, just like a gun.

Moments later, Shirley realized that there was no fuchsia string that lead off in the direction of a far-off tennis ball, only a fuchsia knot tied around the harness. The ball had broken free.

"Well, I'll be. That's a lot of force," Shirley said under her breath, confidence returning. Although she felt bad that she was technically littering, she couldn't muster the energy to hop on her bike and go looking for the wayward ball with 300 yards of string attached to it.

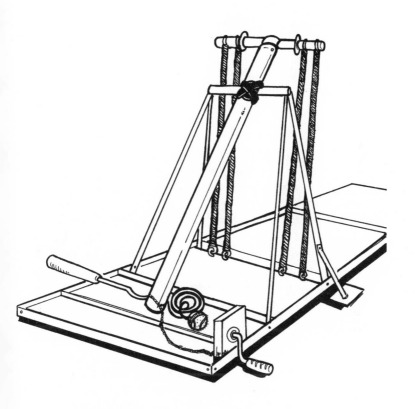

CHAPTER ELEVEN
Overconfidence Shakes Hands with a Bad Idea

Often, progress comes from looking behind or by turning around. A new perspective by being thorough.

"Why?" Shirley asked out loud. "Why put my neighbors at risk? I've got a perfectly good gully to launch tennis balls over. All they'd do is hit the abandoned warehouse." Shirley chastised herself for thinking like an infant. Since the catapult had been built in the garage and the gully was on the other side of the house, it had been out of sight and out of mind. "Why not?" she asked the trunk of a lumbering pine tree. She smacked its trunk for emphasis, its bark rough against her palm.

The risk, she concluded, was acceptable. She'd launch the tennis balls over her house.

Shirley shimmied, shook, scraped, and rotated the catapult as she grunted, flexed, and rested, until it was in position. She turned the catapult 180 degrees and backed it up a couple of feet.

Since she was going to launch blindly over her house and still wanted to make some manner of measurements, Shirley permanent markered each tennis ball with a number. She numbered them sequentially, 1 through 50.

Shirley's physics eyeball was becoming keener along with her physics intuition. The test flight of the first tennis ball was true. It easily cleared the house and flew out of sight in a high arc.

There is something beautiful and calming about a machine that does exactly what it's designed to do, time and time again, like the churning of a washing machine with a full load of clothes or the hypnotic, rhythmic vibration of a clothes dryer. Their motions and functions are soothing, and so was the catapult's. Shirley would load a tennis ball, wind down the winch, hit the release lever, and watch the ball rocket skyward. It would land out of sight, registering the faintest clank of a tennis ball on a tin roof. The sound was so faraway that the impact sounded like something from a dream.

Shirley wasn't bullying nature with her catapult. She was leading it like a dance partner around the floor. Fluid movements. Graceful conversions of stored energy. Fifty in all.

It is difficult to pinpoint where, exactly, the bad idea came from. Maybe it was just lack of raw materials. She found a bright orange fluorescent kid's bowling ball under a pile of rags. An eight or nine pounder. Maybe it was because loading up the pinecones, which whistled eerily, but didn't fly worth a squat hadn't been satisfactory. Maybe it was the glowing satisfaction of an experiment actually working so well she hadn't thought of what do to after its completion. Maybe it was because, with a slight adjustment of the belt on the sling—as simple as cinching a belt on her own pants— the bowling ball fit perfectly into the harness. Maybe it was the tradition of a catapult as a siege engine of war which made it feel like a big ball would complete its design and help realize its original function.

Maybe the bowling ball reminded her of a pumpkin and that's what she really wanted to launch.

But, there it was. A bowling ball, fully winched down, resting on her catapult. A big, bright eye, staring at her. Shirley was hypnotized.

Many spectacular things happened after Shirley was knocked unconscious.

It was a chain reaction. The only warning signal was a

sickening crack.

Nanoseconds after Shirley leaned against the release lever, she realized the load of the bowling ball was too heavy for the throwing arm. The arm exploded like a grenade from the incredible amount of exerted force. Jagged shrapnel flew out like angry, chomping teeth. One piece caught Shirley in the neck, right where her head connected to her shoulder, millimeters away from a thick artery. The metal stuck in her collarbone and a trail of blood followed her as she was knocked back several feet. Other pieces of shrapnel flew through the empty spaces in her baggy clothes when she was staggering backwards. Metal stuck in the brick of her house. Some of it stuck in the trunks of trees. One piece flattened a tire on her car. One piece went through one of the house's front window and shattered a framed portrait of Shirley and Rachel, cutting both their heads off. One deeply cut the tail of a cat, which began screeching in pain and running around in circles before it dashed off to its home. Shirley splayed out on the ground, arms and legs wide, like she was preparing to make a snow angel in the dirt. Her body slowly writhed in pain.

To further complicate matters, the bowling ball had launched at the exact time the metal catastrophically failed and blew apart. The bowling ball flew upwards in a pretty straight line, like an errant baseball slipping from a pitcher's hand. If Shirley had been conscious, she would have seen what looked like a close-by planet hovering above her about to crash into the earth. It was better that Shirley was knocked out because when the bowling ball came back down, when it landed, it broke the upper part of Shirley's left arm in four places. If Shirley had resisted the ball, tensed up and tried to catch it, both of her arms would have been shattered, probably along with bones in her face.

The bowling ball pounded her arm into the soft earth. It didn't roll away. Barely breathing, Shirley's senses, along with her body, were knocked completely flat.

Estelle Tillman, the owner of the cat whose tail had just

been cut, and a former knitting partner of Shirley's, had been gardening four houses down. She'd heard the loud, strange sound. Three things surprised her, in addition to the sound. One, it looked like Shirley's entire front yard had shuddered from some sort of percussion. Two, she knew she was old and her sight wasn't what it used to be and she had been using the lower part of her bifocals to nip the rosebush so it would bloom properly, but she swore she saw a bright orange ball rise and fall back down into Shirley's yard. Three, her cat, Hoover, had zipped by, mewing in pain, and was currently hiding in a nearby tree. As she wiped her knees off, put her hands on her hips, and straightened her back out, she discovered drops of blood on the trunk of the tree as she looked up at Hoover. He remained hidden in high branches thick with leaves, even after she made her most soothing cat sounds. Worried about Hoover, but knowing that there was no such thing as a cat skeleton in a tree, and that he would eventually come down, she first placed a tin of his favorite wet food at the base of the trunk. Estelle then swallowed some of the pride and hurt she'd felt when Shirley quit knitting with her—without the courtesy of a proper goodbye—and walked towards Shirley's house.

After Estelle descended Shirley's driveway and into the front yard, she gasped and crossed herself. She'd never seen a dead person. Well, a person who hadn't died of natural causes. There was full lake of blood around Shirley's head, slightly obscured by the football helmet. There was a bowling ball where part of her arm should have been. Shirley wasn't moving. Estelle didn't fathom that Shirley could still be alive.

Without finishing walking down the driveway, Estelle turned around, rushed back to her house, picked up the phone, and called the police.

In the fifteen minutes that lapsed between the paramedics, police, and firemen department showing up, Shirley's body didn't move. Blood trickled out from her neck.

And in that netherworld, as Shirley's ghost was contemplating being fully formed, Shirley felt ashamed of her selfishness. Even without her body burdening her, feeling light and nimble, free from sags and wrinkles and aches and confusion, a deep spark of humiliation fired inside of her as a man applied pressure on a sterilized bandage to her neck. It wasn't a spark of self-preservation.

Her eyes popped open but she couldn't say a word.

The bowling ball was carefully removed. Paramedics cut her sweater and blouse off with scissors, carefully unearthed her arm and put it in a splint; placed her body on a stretcher, tight, so she couldn't move. She felt secure. They waited for the doctor to remove the football helmet.

It's selfish of me to abandon Rachel, Shirley thought as she tackled her own ghost from behind. I would be cheating my granddaughter of a foundation, of a place to come home to. To family. Don't commit suicide, you dummy, not even in the name of science. What were you thinking? A bowling ball? You know much better. You've got nothing to prove. Think. Think. Think. Stay alive.

These thoughts of Shirley's were solid and real, like they were being indented by the keys of an old typewriter directly into the tissue of her brain.

If I die naturally, she continued to think, that's fine. Just not by your own hand, whatever the justification. Okay? Think. Think. Think. Stay alive.

An oxygen mask was placed over her face, through the bars of the helmet. The paramedics heard the old woman muttering. A needle was inserted into a vein in her right arm. Shirley's thoughts slipped away. A pleasant nothingness wrapped around her like a quilt.

CHAPTER TWELVE
Something Fleshy Yet Bulletproof

As Rachel walked towards her grandmother's house, a full month of summer camp behind her, head and notebook full of new ideas, and an insatiable itch to start experimenting in her own garden, she idly wondered where all of the emergency vehicles were zooming along to. First, a police cruiser, then a fire truck, then an ambulance. They sprayed silty dust from their wheel wells into the air all around the thin sidewalk as they passed, sirens wailing, lights pulsing. Rachel was tired. She stopped and let the dust clouds settle. Although camp had been fun, it'd made her feel rootless and ragged at the edges. She wanted the comfort of sleeping in her bed and listening to familiar sounds, from the clicking on of the rear porch light, to the sound of the wind chimes, to the sound of her grandmother's car as it crunched gravel down the end of the driveway. She missed knowing where everything was in the dark, like the knob of her stereo. She missed the feel of her own garden's soil between her fingers and the opportunity to blast her favorite music out loud and spazz out when Shirley was at work.

As she rounded the final corner to the house, fear jabbed her as quickly, unexpectedly, and repeatedly as a stinging wasp hidden in a sleeping bag.

The emergency vehicles were congregated at the mouth of

her grandmother's driveway. A clot of neighbors was being held at bay by a policeman. Rachel's heart sank further and further with each successive step.

"I'm her granddaughter. I live here. She's my legal guardian," Rachel said matter-of-factly to the mustachioed policeman who held up his hand against her approach. Her eyes didn't betray her. The policeman waved her through, gently grabbed her elbow, and steered her down the driveway. "Watch your step," was the only thing he said.

Rachel's eyes were sponges. They soaked in the entire scene, especially the catapult. Pieces of metal glinted from all over the front yard, looking like scattered tinsel from a blown-up Christmas tree. The front window was shattered. A tire was flat.

It took Rachel fifteen seconds to puzzle together what the detectives were still trying figure out. The catapult was elegant in its simplicity. Skeletal and lean: the machine equivalent to a long distance bicycle rider. How it was designed to function was as pure as its blueprint. All that was missing was its action. Where was the throwing arm that would have used the garage door springs? Rachel thought, as she looked at the straight, black, tightly coiled snakes of metal embedded in the dirt at the ends of short, skidding marks. Then it hit her. All of the pieces of shrapnel and the throwing arm were one in the same. It had blown up.

Then Rachel got scared. She saw a massive, dark puddle that looked like used car oil. It stained the head of what looked like a snow angel fanned into the dirt.

"Blood," she muttered, as tears began to streak down her face. She turned to the policeman. "Where's my grandma?"

The policeman didn't answer and guided her by her elbow to the back of the ambulance.

"Is she okay?" Rachel asked before she could catch a glimpse of Shirley. An EMT climbed down, out of the back of the ambulance, using the bumper as a stair, carefully closing the door behind him so Rachel couldn't see inside. The policeman let go of her arm and walked back up the driveway.

"She's lost a lot of blood and has sustained…."

The EMT said more words, but Rachel didn't hear them. Not again, she thought. No more. Why do all the people I love have to die? she whispered inside her brain. It felt like a black hole had been unzipped from her chest and immediately consumed her body with infinite nothingness. Rachel's legs went weak and she fell backwards. Her arms didn't even move to brace her fall. Luckily, her long backpack padded her impact and protected her head. Before her second bounce against the ground, the EMT scooped her up, scooted her up into the back of the ambulance, sat her on a gurney, removed her backpack, and laid her down in the ambulance opposite her grandmother. He turned to the driver after strapping Rachel in, and yelled, "Let's roll!"

Rachel resumed consciousness twelve hours later. Part of it was shock. Part of it was that she was just really tired. She had been placed in the waiting room, her backpack under her feet. She had stretched out like she was on a lounge chair. All of the hospital beds were full. Rubbing her eyes, she walked towards the nurses' station, yawned deeply, and waited for the woman behind the counter to finish making marks on a clipboard.

"Excuse me," Rachel said. "I'm Shirley Creveling's granddaughter. I came with her in the ambulance." Without prompt, Rachel pulled out her student I.D. and held it out in front of her. Creveling was one of her middle names. There was no mistaking it.

The nurse looked back at her clipboard, took a long look at Rachel, got to her feet, and rounded her desk.

"Follow me," she said without turning around, hearing Rachel's footfalls behind her.

Rachel almost walked right by her grandmother, thinking she was on the other side of a curtain that separated the room in two, when the nurse made a smart, fast turn, looked up to a machine with a digital readout, and said, "She just got out of surgery. She's still unconscious. You can only be a minute. She's got to rest."

With all of the tubes and machines and the plastic mask over her face and the thicket of bandages at her neck and her entire right arm hidden away, like a caterpillar in a bright white cocoon, Rachel had to look twice and then stare. The person underneath all that effort of medicine sure didn't look like her grandmother.

"Oh," she whispered, as she recognized Shirley's hair. Then she recognized the wrinkles around Shirley's eyes and the lines at the edges of her mouth from her easy smile.

Rachel x-rayed through the tangle of tubes and Shirley looked puffy and drained of blood. She looked like an old, dented car that had been hit in an accident, patched with body filler, then sterilized. Shirley didn't move.

A machine blipped in a steady rhythm, confirming a heartbeat.

"She's been through a lot," the nurse said. "The old gal's got a lot of fight in her." The nurse's voice was detached yet had a hint of admiration pocketed behind it.

"Will she be okay?" Rachel asked, fear creeping up her throat and choking her.

"She's got a lot of fight in her," the nurse repeated, neither confirming nor denying what she'd been asked.

Rachel reached down and touched her grandmother's good hand. It was warm. Looking closely, she could see blood thrum through the veins on the back of Shirley's hand, and this gave her comfort. Maybe her grandmother just needed a long rest. Rachel knew Shirley was tough. Those guys who work out at the gym, with veiny muscles exploding all over the place—that's how Rachel imagined her grandmother's heart. Something fleshy yet bulletproof. Something that could take hammering and shock and still flex in and out and carry a tremendous weight easily, like it was as heavy as a Ping Pong ball.

CHAPTER THIRTEEN
Twenty-One Days of Heartbeats

When Rachel returned to the house, alone, new holes and a flat tire greeted her. The front door was locked and she keyed herself in. She sat down, semi-paralyzed. Fear, sadness, and immediate loneliness crumpled her like a page torn out of a book, wadded up, and thrown on the floor. A crinkled ball of feelings got fisted up inside of Rachel. She wanted to cry. She also wanted to fix everything. She wanted to walk up to strangers and start yelling at them. All at the same time. Slowly, she got to the business of cleaning up the house and yard. Her brain relaxed as her muscles took over the thinking for awhile.

There was still a month left of summer before school started. Every morning, Rachel would get on her bike and pedal to the hospital. At first, the empty house was creepy. She'd never been in it for more than a couple of hours without her grandmother, but even the way Rachel boiled water or sat in the Lay-Z-Boy, the thumbprints of her grandmother's advice and existence were all around her, almost as real as her human hands.

Rachel limited herself to one project each day. First, she vacuumed all of the glass from the front room. Then she removed the shards of broken glass, rode her bike into town, got a replacement pane, and installed it.

Using the spanner and jack, she removed the car wheel with

the flat tire, put it in Shirley's garage sale cart that she'd made as a trailer for her bicycle, and got it patched.

The round, dark patch of blood in the dirt of the front yard disturbed her. Several times, she hit it with the hose, hoping it would dissipate. It didn't. With trowel in a slightly shaking hand, she dug into the blood spot, turning the soil. She'd purchased a rose bush. She wanted it to bud as soon as possible, and she planted it dead center in the middle of Shirley's spilt blood. Something good had to bloom from that spot. It wasn't a gravesite; Rachel was convinced. She wanted to look out of the front of the house and see something pretty. Something that made her think happy thoughts, and not of a machine that might have killed her grandmother.

After all of the repairs were done to the house and all of the metal that could be removed was thrown in the trash, Rachel planted some seeds in the garden. These were the first seeds Rachel planted with a new body of knowledge. They were the same types of seeds she'd been using before, but how her brain was studying them and monitoring them; that was the difference.

The first two weeks of visits were grim. Shirley didn't wake up. She didn't move. All of her vital signs were steady and her body was repairing itself slowly, heartbeat by heartbeat.

All Rachel could do was hold her grandmother's hand and look at her in her sleep. When the nurses weren't around, she'd place her ear near her grandmother's chest. The heartbeat was a comfort. Rachel also learned from the doctor about Shirley's arm and the bowling ball that had crushed it—compound fractures clean through both bones in her lower arm: radius and ulna. She also learned about the piece of metal that grazed within an eighth of an inch of her carotid artery, and that she could have bled to death in a matter of minutes if that had been severed. It was a tremendous amount of trauma if it'd happened to a young and healthy person, the doctor had said. Catastrophe loomed. Shirley's age was a liability.

It's a hell of a price to pay for the good luck of not dying, Rachel was thinking on the fifteenth day, moments before her grandmother's eyes softly opened and her hand squeezed Rachel's.

"Hey," Rachel said softly. "Nice to have you back." Her eyes swelled with tears.

Shirley smiled very slightly, put a little more pressure into her squeeze, then let go. She fell back asleep. Shirley's smile remained and that sustained Rachel's hope.

Each day after was a baby step of improvement. Eyes open a little bit longer. A tighter hand squeeze. Twenty-one days after being thrown into a pool of her own blood, Shirley said her first words.

"I shouldn't have done that."

"Done what?" Rachel asked.

"The catapult."

"That's a great looking machine, Grandma."

"It almost killed me."

"What happened?"

Slowly, deliberately, Shirley took Rachel through all of the steps. Penitent and paying for the sins of not telling Rachel the whole truth in the responses to her postcards, Shirley tried to not let any detail slip her memory. It took over an hour. She even told Rachel about the man shotgunning beers off of the jackalope head before he knocked over her stop sign pole.

"I'm not passing judgement," Rachel said, "but you shouldn't have loaded up that bowling ball."

Shirley chortled, which turned into a wet, hacking rasp. "I think you're right."

"So the throwing arm just exploded?"

"Like a grenade. Maybe using a stop sign wasn't the best idea after all."

There was a long silence. Rachel didn't have any advice. She would have probably loaded up the bowling ball, too. It was there. Experiments often call for bold moves.

"How're you feeling?"

"Torn in two, but stitched back together. I couldn't stand the thought of leaving you alone."

Rachel let her eyes drop their gaze. Tears fell silently. "Thanks for not dying, Grandma. I don't know what I'd do to myself if you left without saying goodbye…. Mom never got to say hello."

On the thirtieth day, one day before Rachel started her junior year of high school, Shirley was released. Although the stitches were still in place, her neck had healed and the newest x-ray confirmed that her bones were knitting back together and setting. She could read again without losing her place or getting a headache. That was a tremendous relief.

Shirley immediately noticed the rose bush in the front yard. It had the smallest of green buds at the tips of its brown, thorny branches. It had grown at an amazing rate. Her gaze went from it, directly to Rachel's eyes. "Thank you."

In the quiet of the evening, when soup was simmering on the stove, and Rachel was fussing over the spices, cautiously taking mouth-cooled sips off of a large wooden spoon, Shirley turned to her granddaughter. "I think I'm done."

"Done with what?" Rachel asked.

"Done tinkering around."

The last thing Rachel wanted to do was disagree with her grandmother about big things in her life, so she lent a soft, emotional shoulder. "I'm sorry to hear that. You were getting really good at it. But, I think I understand."

A month later, the outside stitches were removed; Shirley's neck was pink and pinched and raised. The cast was carefully sawn off, the plaster splitting down the middle. It wasn't until Shirley was in the shower and had carefully cleaned off all the grayness that had settled between the cast and her skin that she became completely demoralized. At first, it didn't make any sense. Letters were impressed on her forearm, and they were backwards. Y F F E J.

And then it struck her, as hard as that fateful bowling ball. It was the name that had been inscribed into the ball itself, a kid's ball. A kid by the name of J E F F Y. The indignity of being fifty-nine years old and having equivalent of a bad tattoo in a highly conspicuous place was too much.

"I'm done. I'm done. I'm done." Shirley said to her reflection in the mirror.

And for the next six months she was. When her health was better, she disassembled the rusting catapult completely. Every week, she would fill her trash barrel with as much of it that would fit, until it was merely a memory.

Then, for six months after that, one moth of anxiety after another flitted through Shirley's cathedral of peace and quiet, of knitting and unfettered work. She tried to ignore them. She knitted exquisite and complicated sweaters while mastering new patterns. She quilted the biggest and best afghans of her entire life. But even with her fingers occupied, her mind dipped and twirled. The dance of physics was curtseying, extending its hand, and entreating her to join.

It would only be a matter of time, Shirley knew, before she'd be back to her experiments.

CHAPTER FOURTEEN
The Secret Life of Hairspray

Slingshot, bomb, or missile? Shirley thought, bobbling between the three images. She thought it'd be better to keep quiet for a bit. Sleep longer.

And then it came to her. Combustion. Propulsion. Tool shed thermodynamics. Capturing the essence of an explosion. A kind bomb or a good missile. She smelled her granddaughter's hairspray. That was the answer to a question not yet asked. That was the ignition.

Shirley smiled a wicked, inflated smile. She turned to her granddaughter and with a grin that looked too large for her mouth, said, "Hairspray."

"What did you say?"

"Hairspray, hairspray, hairspray." Shirley's voice was elated, singsong.

Rachel didn't really know how to respond.

"Hairspray!" Shirley exclaimed.

After Shirley convalesced, it was the perfect time and excuse to completely bow out of Chamber of Commerce functions, stealthily neglect baking cookie squares, and never attend another knitting group ever again. She was like a low-flying Cessna, dipping from the community's radar. It was a barely detected disappearance. As was said before, Shirley didn't leave that much of an impression on people. She wasn't on their thoughts that often. To them, it was like Shirley had gotten up to use the bathroom and never came back. They knew she'd been in an accident, put little else.

As Shirley stepped back from those obligations, she saw a large strand of her life that she had previously discarded, like a used umbilical cord. Not even fully aware of the nourishment that experimentation would provide, purpose began to creep back into her life, then, suddenly, it was like a muzzle flash of light and flame.

Before long, even with a full work schedule resuming, Shirley had this alien thing on her hands. Free time. The next five months seemed to pass as quickly as a series of developing Polaroid pictures. Secret Project Hairspray was the name of the project. Rachel was the only other soul who knew about it. Shirley wanted to punch the world back good. She'd never thought of it before: destruction could be creative. She wanted to strike back, precisely, without collateral damage. Make a big, ol' sweater of damage; nice and neat and as functional as a box stitch.

Shirley re-embraced her nascent hobby: practical engineering. Mixing physics in, she became fascinated with fuel ratios, ignition systems, thermodynamics, velocities, trajectories, and optimum barrel lengths. At first, all of these newish concepts danced in her head like an awkward partner; its feet moved stiffly and the two didn't know where to put their hands on each other. Awkward jolts of not knowing how to solve a problem would wash over her, but she stayed at her task through endless pencils and the rapid tapping of a calculator. At first, her brain ached something fierce. Numbers and patterns slowly opened up and revealed themselves.

Again, it was the invisible stuff that intrigued Shirley. She was convinced that if she could see what others couldn't and then make something that they all could see, but not quite believe, well, that was the stuff of Newton and Einstein. "When people pull something from what looks like thin air," Shirley muttered to herself, "there's real power in that."

She had cleared out a part of the garage, cleaned up ten feet of bench space, and installed more lighting. She made sure her chair was at the right height to stave off fatigue. Whenever she was at a thinking pause, she'd reach over and insert her pencil in the electric sharpener, hoping that it would also shave her ideas into a fine point.

Wanting to commit as much to paper as possible, she noted every little detail. Every possible variable. Not long after, Shirley had a thick notebook crammed full of diagrams, theories, and plans. Hairspray was the catalyst.

CHAPTER FIFTEEN
Deflating Like a Balloon Animal

The guy at the hardware store, Chet, thought Shirley was helping her husband install a sprinkler system for a garden. Although Shirley made sure she didn't lie to the salesman, she let him use his own assumptions without correction. Chet also thought Shirley's measurements and thicknesses were completely out of whack. He wished her husband would have just come instead, thinking that Shirley had muddled it all up.

"Four inch in diameter water pipe, ma'am, that's mighty wide. Are you sure?" Chet asked, trying to keep his cool. He already had visions of the woman returning mud-soaked pipe and expecting a full refund. It wouldn't have been the first time.

Making note of his nametag, Shirley nodded and announced the next item, ticking the four-inch pipe off her list.

Chet was annoyed. What she was getting, Chet thought, wouldn't water dickall. "Ma'am," Chet asked, his voice rising in irritation because he thought he was helping Shirley out, "You don't really need the pressure-rated PVC pipe. Regular pipe'll hold up just fine for regular watering purposes."

Shirley squinted and pushed her glasses back to the bridge of her nose in thought. She didn't mean to be condescending. "I've studied up on polyvinyl chloride." Yet, Chet's suggestion spurred a new idea. "You wouldn't have any clear PVC, would you? That'd be pretty."

Chet smiled back a fuck you. Lady, he thought, you're a dip-shit. Yet, his lips moved in a professional manner and he said, "No, no. I don't suppose we do. But the pressure rated pipe's more expensive."

"I figured as much. That's what I'll need, though." Shirley inspected the pipe that Chet had placed in the cart. It had the correct markings inked on the side.

Chet tugged at his yellow smock. "What else you got?"

With each subsequent item from the list, Chet resembled a balloon animal being slowly deflated. He'd prided himself in getting people what they needed—prided in presupposing their projects—and he was much more often right than wrong. This lady had baffled him into a state of despondency. He could sort of understand the bushings, adapters, threaded plugs, couplers, primer, and pipe cement—although all put together they'd make a fat, functionless anaconda of a sprinkler system. This lady's screwed, Chet thought.

"Chet, I'm looking for a barbecue igniter, the type used for a grill with a side burner—a two pole igniter—if possible."

With that, Chet was back in the game. He liked things in his store that sparked, blew up, or had some velocity to them. "Yes ma'am. We've got several to chose from, but they all come in one color." Shirley inspected the four different igniters. One caught her fancy. It was piezoelectric. She clicked it several times, very quickly, studying the spark plug-like zap of ignition.

"Chet, did you know that the word 'piezo' is Greek for 'push'? So what I'm going to buy is 'pressure electric.'"

"Hadn't given it any thought. Well, that ain't exactly true," Chet said. "They're always comin' up with new names for old things so I stopped paying attention. It still lights barbecues plenty good. I know that."

"Oh, it's very old," Shirley said. "Piezoelectricity was discovered by two brothers when they were both in their twenties—

Pierre and Jacques Curie—a little over a hundred years ago. 1880 or so." Chet's eyes had already glazed over so Shirley kept the tidbit to herself about how the development of a charge on a crystal is proportional to the pressure, and that's what made the lighter work so efficiently. A piece of quartz made the spark. It further fascinated Shirley that the same technology worked in microphones, too. She kept that to herself also. "That'll be it. Thanks."

Chet swung around to get behind the register. Before he scanned the first item, he looked Shirley squarely in the blindingly fluorescent green sweater that had a reindeer knitted in the middle, which, in turn had a pompom for a nose, and said, "Ma'am, you're aware of our ten percent re-stocking fee for any returned items?" It occurred to Chet that he hadn't looked directly at the lady once during their entire interaction.

"You bet," Shirley said, confident in her purchases. "Oh, and these, too." She reached into a bin and placed some spicy cinnamon candy on the belt along with all the parts Chet had helped her find.

CHAPTER SIXTEEN
Ducks and Rabbits on Ether

When Shirley got home, she rushed back and forth, unloading all of the materials. The top of her head tingled with excitement, like tiny snakes radiating from her scalp.

Rachel looked up from her homework as her grandma burst through the front door. The two had made a pact. Shirley wanted to keep all of the formative experiments to herself, to complete the first steps of the research and development, so she could have a solid idea formulated. She wanted to keep her mistakes private.

Rachel had little idea what her grandma was attempting and whenever Shirley was in the garage, Rachel gave her space. Plus, Shirley had given Rachel a project all her own. Rachel had been working hard on that.

To ease from the world of pure theory—of penciled numbers and symbols on pieces of graph paper—to the actual, real, physical pieces of pipe, Shirley very carefully laid out everything. These pieces were the disconnected bones of the idea. Shirley's brain and hands would give it muscle, give it a function, give it a purpose beyond a loose collection of parts that had been separated in bins until hours before. Shirley also installed a paper towel dispenser, close at the ready, for any small spills. She was ultra prepared. Broken bones will do that.

Shirley was acutely aware of what she was about to attempt was no history in the making. In fact, the Floridian man who had sold her his crude plans for ten dollars through the mail was also selling "How to make you own 40 oz. beer coozie with carpet padding" instructions, Molly Hatchet live bootleg cassettes, and tips on the finer points of alligator wrestling ("Gittin' bit's no fun. It's like having a car door studded with nails slam on yer arm."). Shirley wanted to ease into the hard stuff and figured that if a charming man, whose plans were one step above crayons on a napkin—but structurally solid—hadn't killed himself yet, that she had a good chance of repeating the results. Ease into the hard stuff. Building blocks.

After carefully measuring and marking, she got down to cutting, filing, and chamfering the edges of the PVC. She stripped the barbecue igniter's wires, drilled holes, screwed in screws, and soldered wires into place. Before using any solvents, she snugged parts together and then pulled them back apart with a thwong.

Knowing that minutes of extra care during construction would prevent the material from prematurely fatiguing, or the whole operation blowing apart, she inspected the threads of the PVC seams under a magnifying glass. She drew a small triangle file back and forth between the threads, removing small burrs, and carefully razor-blading out the slightest bit of plastic at the bottom of each groove. Knitting had undoubtedly helped with the precision. Shirley tested the cleanout cap with a twist. It practically threaded itself.

Carefully, using a constant sweeping motion for consistent coverage, she applied the primer to a female PVC fitting. She did the same to the male fitting, pushed them together, and held them in place for thirty seconds, to make sure the union wouldn't break apart under stress. She continued this procedure many times and a contiguous object began to appear in front of her.

Shirley had never done drugs, but she had no trouble realizing that she was high for the first time in her life as her head dipped and bobbed from all of the pipe glue solvent she had daubed onto the pipe while curing the barrel. The garage had no ventilation, no circulation, save for tiny slice of cool air that came from under the side door. As all the individual parts were liquefying, intertwining, and rehardening into a joined piece of plastic by PVC polymers, Shirley remembered a long-ago cartoon about ducks and rabbits, bounding around on ether, talking very slurrily. For all the effort she took in trying to form words, none came out. She felt like an underwater diver. No motion came quickly. She felt restricted, as if encased in a rubber suit. She also felt disturbed, like somebody had magically taken off her underwear and then put them back on, over all her clothes. She was maddened at how slowly her body moved and how vividly depicted the loud ducks and rabbits hopped and quacked all around her as she turned the knob, threw the door open to the outside, and breathed in deep lungs of cold, sweet air. When she looked down and was able to gather her thoughts, she was pleased to see that her bra and panties were still where she'd originally put them when she'd gotten dressed that morning.

After a couple of minutes, she was much better, save for the onset of a headache. The fumes from the glue had passed like a storm through her brain, streaking gray clouds through it, while pulling curtains over the deeper thoughts she was attempting. She was discombobulated. As she walked back to her creation, an occasional whiff streaked through her senses, quick as lightning.

"Ol' gal," Shirley said to herself, "using glue without ventilation isn't rocket science. It's common sense."

With the door open, the temperature in the garage plummeted. Shirley carefully studied her creation from all angles. She scrutinized the seams. She triple measured lengths. Clapping her hands against the cold, she sucked some air between her teeth. Her arm hurt. All things considered, the device was looking how she'd designed it to. She'd have to wait twenty-four hours for the solvent fumes to dissipate and all the parts to properly cure. Shirley was patient. She knew that, done correctly, solvent welds in plastic were stronger than metal welds. Well, that's what she'd read.

She closed up shop for the night and pulled the balled chain to turn off the racks of fluorescent lights overhead.

Rachel looked up from her botany book as her grandmother returned from the garage. "How'd it go?" she asked.

"Too early to tell," Shirley responded, "and I don't want to jinx it, but I should know in the next couple of days."

"So soon?"

"Don't want to jinx it," Shirley repeated. "What are your thoughts on some cheese potato soup?"

Rachel looked at her grandmother, who took off her boots and put on some slippers. She padded into the kitchen.

"I was wondering why you got so many potatoes." Rachel elbowed up from the couch and looked at the ten-pound bags. "Five bags. Were they on sale?"

Shirley smiled and frowned at the same time. "Yes." She didn't, technically, lie to her granddaughter, because they had been on sale, but potato soup hadn't been the main reason for the purchase, not by a long shot. Rachel would know soon, Shirley thought.

Shirley commenced to make a cheese potato soup, accenting it with fried onion topping and additional shredded cheese. She made enough so both of them could fill up their vacuum flasks and take it for lunch the next day. Vacuum flasks? Shirley had felt a creeping, but solid change in herself. The things she had previously taken for granted, she now looked into. All around her was a flowering of curiosity, as bright and full as the rose bush in the front yard. Invented by Sir James Dewar, a scientist in England, the outer container of the flask is separated by the inner container by a vacuum. "Hot stays hot, cold stays cold," Shirley said to herself. "Thermos is just the German trade name."

"What was that, grandma?" Rachel craned her neck to the

kitchen.

Shirley hadn't realized that she'd been talking to herself. "Oh… I was thinking of making a lot. So you can take some to school tomorrow."

"Sure. That sounds good." Rachel went back to reading her book.

CHAPTER SEVENTEEN
Stroked Carefully, Like a Wild Animal

Two days later, Shirley began talking to her left foot as she drove home. "No need to speed," she said to her foot as it eased off the accelerator. "Let's not get hasty. No one else has to be put in jeopardy." As soon as she parked the station wagon, she continued talking, this time to her still tender arm and leg. "Take your time," she said as she conscientiously put more weight on the weaker leg, careful not to trip over a rock or slip on wet leaves. The leg had healed, but it still felt like it was on loan to someone else. It didn't quite feel like her own. The J E F F Y arm ached almost all the time.

After the fluorescent lights in the garage fizzed to life and blinked on, she carefully touched her invention. With gaining confidence, she ran her fingers over the almost imperceptible seams. She stared down the barrel. It was smooth, white, and shiny. The whole thing felt solid. Nothing was wonky. Pulling up the stool, she got to work on finishing the installation of the ignition. When she briskly depressed the plunger, a bright spark snapped as it jumped between two carefully positioned screws twisted into the PVC. She did this fifteen more times. Each time, a sharp spark crackled and pirouetted on cue. "Science can be so beautiful," she said to herself.

*　　*　　*

Shirley was ready for a practical test. She put in a pair of earplugs, opened the side door, pulled down a can of hairspray, and popped off the cap.

The she stopped. "No. Not again."

She hesitated, then battled against herself. "Do it."

Palms sweating, she jammed a clean shop rag down into the barrel of the PVC tube with a broomstick. At the other end, where there was a chamber, she dispensed a few seconds of hairspray, then quickly closed the chamber with an endcap. Swiveling in her chair, not expecting much of a show of force, but bracing herself just the same, she pointed the launcher at a folded-up Ping Pong table at the far end of the garage. Holding the launcher firmly with both hands, she depressed the barbecue plunger. With a very loud report, a flaming rag flew across the garage and knocked a clock clean off the wall. Shirley was jolted back. She regained her footing and smiled. She placed the homemade gun back on the work bench, walked across the garage, stomped the flames out of the rag, and was lifting the shattered clock up when Rachel rushed through the door.

"Are you okay? I heard a loud noise! What's that smell?" Rachel's gaze started at the broken clock in her grandmother's hands but was lured away by the gleaming white plastic gun on the workbench.

"I'm better than okay," Shirley beamed. "I'm fantastic." She paused. "A rag caught fire. My fault," Shirley said when she realized that using a flammable projectile was pretty dumb. Who'd ever heard of a rag damaging anything, Shirley thought, no matter how hard it was thrown?

"This is what you've been making? It's smaller than I thought it would be," Rachel said as she looked at the gun, careful not to touch it. "You've lugged a bunch of bags into the garage."

"It's more powerful than I thought it'd be," Shirley said, removing the earplugs and stealthily crumbling up the ashes of the shop rag with her foot. "I have enough material to make a couple more. This one's the prototype." Her hands were throbbing. Bones ached along previous breaks.

"Do you want to know how it works... well, how it's supposed to work? I haven't really kicked the tires on it. Just revved the engine a little."

Rachel nodded.

Before she gave her granddaughter a tour of the launcher, she wanted Rachel to understand the basic principles of firearms.

"It's really very simple. You see, the very first firearms were little more than a chamber with a big hole in one end and a little hole in the other. The powder and projectile were jammed down the big end. Fire was put on the little end, then, pop! This is the same idea with a couple important modifications: potato in one end; fire in the other. What I've done is make a barrel for the potato and placed where the fire comes from behind it. I made it that way for other reasons, too; so a potato can't be jammed up against the igniter and muck it up." Shirley continued, describing the full theory, the basic components of the barrel, fuel chamber, and ignition system, how to load it, how it all worked, and the safety precautions. As she did, she made Rachel touch the device. Rachel tentatively stroked it like it was a live, undomesticated animal. "Point it," Shirley emphasized, "only at what you want to destroy." It was still in perfect condition. There was only the smallest trace of soot on the inside of the barrel. Her craftsmanship had held. She let Rachel pick it up, feel the weight of it, and finished up with, "It all started with hairspray," Shirley said. "That's what got me to thinking."

Rachel carefully placed the gun back on the workbench. "Grandma, I didn't think I'd ever say this about a gun, but I'm proud of you."

CHAPTER EIGHTEEN
A Pornographically Loud Sound

After dinner, the two of them looked at each other. Both could virtually read one another's thoughts as easily as comic strip word balloons.

"Grandma, do you want to do some launching tonight? That's really why you bought all of those, right?" Rachel eyed the sacks of potatoes in the kitchen.

"It's only a quarter moon tonight," Shirley responded, "We wouldn't be able to see how far the spuds go."

"What about cutting up some glow sticks and covering the potatoes with their fluid? That way we'd be able to see where they end up."

"Like a tracer round." Shirley was pleased that she had such an inventive granddaughter, but she was still more than a little nervous. She wondered if her launcher could take a potato or if the gun would explode in her hands and cripple her for good. "Mind if I take the first shot?"

"You made the thing," Rachel said. "I'm standing back this time." Rachel still felt awful about screwing up her grandmother's leg.

Before long, the two were in the back yard, overlooking the ravine. The paper mill was inked in complete darkness, erased from sight. "We can probably do three or four before the neighbors think something's amiss," Shirley whispered.

"I don't think you need to whisper," Rachel said as held a flashlight to the just-cracked light stick to make the goo as bright as possible. It glowed a vivid, yet soft, neon green, which matched Shirley's sweater. After a few minutes, Rachel sliced open the stick, drizzled the fluid over a potato resting on newspaper, then handed it to her grandma. Shirley shoved the crisp potato down the tube, using the broomstick to shove it further down. The potato created a nice seal as it was forced down the barrel. She breathed deeply. "Okay, honey. Please step back." Shirley sprayed the hairspray in, recapped the chamber, gripped the launcher, and twisted her feet into the ground for stability right before she pushed down on the igniter.

The sound was pornographically loud. It was as if a jet was taking off from their backyard. The roar was followed by a six-foot tongue of blue flame from the barrel as the neon green spud zipped through the darkness like a rocket. Rachel followed its flight—a bright, eerily straight thread of light—for little more than a second. Then it disappeared. Two hollow kwoonnngggs reverberated back a couple seconds later.

"Shit, grandma," Rachel exclaimed. "Holy shoot," Rachel said, automatically correcting her language.

"Dang butt!" Shirley exclaimed at almost the same time.

Shirley tucked her head down and gritted her teeth in embarrassment for making so much noise, trying to slink away and doing a little dance of realization that she'd just gotten the attention of the entire neighborhood. "Uhhh, I think one's okay for now. Let's get back inside the house." Shirley's mind was reeling.

"Dang, grandma. What is that thing?"

Shirley was shaking from nerves and the recoil. Not only did she have the puma of physics, she had just put her head into its jaws. Unexpectedly, a wave of dissatisfaction flowed over her as they quietly hurried inside the house and she placed the launcher back in the garage. Its barrel was warm to the touch. It smelled vaguely of french fries.

"The potato provided just the right amount of resistance. The sides of it are wet, so it forms a seal. All of the hairspray had to go somewhere when it was ignited."

"Did you think it'd be that powerful?" Rachel asked.

"I wasn't quite sure," Shirley's voice was infused with dejection. She really didn't care how loud or how fiery the launcher was. "The potato barely made it to the mill... I really haven't improved upon the catapult."

"You're kidding me, right?" Rachel looked at her grandma's droopy face.

"What are you saying?" Shirley asked. "That potato went through the siding."

"You don't have to make me feel better. The potato just hit the side, just like those rocks or tennis balls."

"That potato, grandma, not only went through the siding facing us, I think it went all the way through the warehouse."

Shirley thought her granddaughter was only trying to be nice.

"Tomorrow, let's go take a look," Rachel offered. "It'll be Saturday."

Shirley agreed only after having waited an hour. No police cruisers came trolling by. The neighborhood was once again still.

CHAPTER NINETEEN
Soreness Feeling Like Accomplishment

With a mug of hot cocoa, heat tonguing up and fogging her glasses as she sipped it, Shirley watched the sunrise from her back porch. Her eyes were heavy and she was tired, but her body responded to a deeply imbedded sleep routine which got her up at six. In her fitful sleep, dejection and elation had seesawed up and down; on one end was a cartoony puma, silent; on the other side were evil clowns with rotting teeth, bad breath, and terrible jokes.

Rachel, in her PJs and a heavy coat, took one step out into the cold.

"Hon, I made some cocoa for you," Shirley said as she looked back at the sound of the door opening.

"Thanks." Rachel put some extra marshmallows on the top, then stepped out again. "Grandma, even if I'm wrong about the potato, I'm so proud of you."

The two looked at the old paper mill. It was massive.

"So," Shirley asked, "you want to walk over there with me?"

Rachel negotiated a sip around a melting marshmallow. "You bet. Let me get some real clothes on."

It was a time of firsts for Shirley. She had never trespassed before. To the best of her memory, she hadn't climbed a fence in over twenty-five years. Shirley was pleased that she scaled it with only a little difficulty, and she could even lift herself completely up over the sharp barbs at the top without snagging anything. When they walked through the muddy field toward the mill, it occurred to her that wearing a bright orange sweater probably wasn't the stealthiest way to go about breaking the law.

They easily found the section of the mill they were looking for. It was the only section that was severely dented. Scattered rocks lay conspicuously about. "I guess it wouldn't be too difficult to figure where most of these came from," Shirley said as she swiveled her head and saw the back of her house in the distance.

Rachel found the hole without much effort. A curlicue of potato shaving confirmed her guess. The hole's edges were cleanly flanged. The surrounding metal paneling wasn't dented in. That potato had continued hauling ass right through the siding, just as Rachel thought. She peered through the two-inch-wide hole. About fifty feet away was a small foreman's shed, made from the same material. She thought she could see the potato splatted against it. She was pretty sure of her discovery. The inside of the warehouse was also peppered with bright green tennis balls.

Rachel began doing a happy little pogo, up and down.

Shirley continued inspecting the siding with her eyes. "Rache, you found anything?"

Rachel continued bopping up and down, hoping to get her grandmother's attention without saying a word.

"Rache," Shirley turned around. "You found it?"

Rachel pointed to the hole.

"You sure?"

Rachel answered by bobbing her head and pouting her lips to a song she was singing to herself in her head.

Shirley walked up and immediately stuck several fingers into the hole. The potato shaving was unmistakable. "Oh, my," she said as she backed up and looked through the hole. "Oh my. Is that it, over there?" Shirley pointed through the hole to what looked like

101

a smashed potato in the distance.

"I'm thinking so," Rachel beamed. "Told you I heard it go through."

There was no easy way they could get to inspect the potato more closely, but the evidence was conclusive.

Shirley blushed with pride. She'd done it. According to her data, that potato had a muzzle velocity in excess of four hundred miles per hour.

"Yeee!" she squealed. "Are those my tennis balls too?" She answered her own question with another extended "Yeee!"

Shirley mimicked her granddaughter's dance. They both pogoed and swung their heads back and forth in jubilation. Rachel played air guitar, stopping briefly for the occasional solo, kicking rocks as she pretended to tap the reverb pedal with her foot.

They both practically floated home.

Shirley thought of fields where they could partake in a little target practice and began to make a checklist in her head of all the stuff to take.

"You up for some science?" Shirley asked coyly, knowing the answer.

"As long as we can take some stuff that'll blow up," Rachel answered.

Two hours later, the sum total of carnage that hairspray, PVC pipe, raw potatoes, and American ingenuity had wreaked was impressive.

The two had driven ten minutes out of town. The firing range was littered with debris.

The launcher didn't blow up. It fired predictably.

The women's aim wasn't perfect, since they'd never fired a weapon—and actually aimed it at something smaller than an entire warehouse—prior to that day, yet they adapted quickly, especially considering there was neither a front nor rear sight, just eyeballing.

An old toaster lie in ruin. Paint cans filled with water exploded in backflipping cascades. A broken keyboard was punished with a direct hit, its keys chittered away in pulses.

With each safely administered, carefully documented shot, Shirley was already thinking of refinements as her notebook filled up with numbers, ideas, symbols, and formulae. Fortuitously, they ran out of targets and potatoes at the same time they ran out of hairspray.

"This can't be legal," Rachel said jokingly. "It's way too much fun." She, too, was hooked.

Shirley made another note about the questionable legality of their activity and wrote the single word "firearm" on the page. She followed it with a long sequence of question marks.

The accumulation of recoil left them both sore, but the soreness felt like accomplishment.

"Grandma, you made a quality gun, there," Rachel said, tapping the barrel. "Would you like some help painting it?"

Shirley was bending down, picking up the larger shattered chunks of the toaster. "That'd be nice. But, could you wait a bit? I want to work on some improvements before we pretty it up."

"Sure."

"How's that pumpkin project coming along?" Shirley asked.

"Good, I think," replied Rachel. "I'm already working on growing three or four different types. Already cross breeding them. A variety called Pankow's Field has a smoother, thicker rind, less of a seed cavity, and more flesh. Connecticut Field is small and round, like a globe. One called an Oz Hybrid has an ultra smooth shell. Things are shaping up." Rachel had remembered how her grandma asked for pumpkins that were hard, round, and smooth, without explaining why. Now she understood. She wanted pumpkins like bullets, not pumpkins for pie.

"Oh," Shirley said, "I had no idea you'd done so much work on it. Those are all types of pumpkins?"

"You're not the only one who's been sneaking around," Rachel said. "Plus, it's a little more interesting than studying French."

"Sí," Shirley responded.

CHAPTER TWENTY
Boom! Boom! Boom!

Another cluster of months passed, and with each, a series of improvements to the potato launcher, which was always thoroughly cleaned and re-inspected for cracks and discoloration after a full afternoon of activity. They also cleaned out the mashed and caked-on Russets.

Comfort came first. Shirley relocated the bazooka-like ignition switch into a more traditional pistol grip. Her inspiration came at a stoplight. The wind was whipping that day. It drew Shirley's attention to a large street sign, which swayed over the middle of the street. The sign hung from a metal arm attached to the traffic signal pole. The sign was attached to the arm by tough, resilient metal clamps, attached by what looked like handles. The configuration of the handles gave Shirley an idea. She took a left, drove to the hardware store, and once again baffled Chet with her selection of parts.

By sawing down a PVC tee, fastening it to a block of wood, positioning two small screws, and wrapping a clothespin with copper wire to make an electronic trigger, it only took a couple hours. Shirley reveled in the craftsmanship. Knitting's rewards, although ample, were often too quiet. Shirley thrilled when her new trigger fired perfectly after she hose clamped it to the combustion chamber. She attached another handle for more stability. The grand total for the handles cost about four dollars. They definitely made the potatoes fly out of the launcher that much more predictably.

"Boom! Boom! Boom!" Shirley mouthed as hundreds of potatoes flew from of the muzzle.

At first, Shirley didn't notice the dig of the launcher's recoil into her hands, between her thumb and forefinger, where the hose clamp had bitten her many times during the weekend's research and development. She felt self-conscious at work, with noticeable and oddly positioned cuts. Knitting, once again, came to the rescue and found an appropriate place on the gun. Starting in the middle of the week on her breaks, she knitted what everyone who passed her in the lunchroom suspected were booties for a little girl. In reality, they were handle covers—bright pink—which effectively dampened the recoil, protected the shooter's hands, and prevented them from being cut again by the hose clamps. They also muted some of the "gunliness" of the launcher, which was important to Shirley.

At twenty-five years of unquestioned dedication to her job, Shirley had been awarded a plaque and a laser pointer. The laser pointer was a conundrum, since Shirley rarely gave speeches, and none of those speeches had anything to be pointed at. She figured the government just had a surplus, but she kept the laser anyway. The plaque remained on her cubicle's wall and gathered a fine felt of dust on its top edge, but she had plans for the pointer.

She fashioned a housing for the pointer on the launcher, made sure it was lined up perfectly with the barrel, and attached it to the top of the gun. It worked like a charm on gray days or near dark. She would have thought it was almost too easy, shooting at the random grouping of lawn ornaments she'd picked up garage saling the weekend before, but she couldn't hold back her delight as parts of their bodies exploded in a white, plastery mist. Shirley was both scared and exhilarated, illuminating a little red dot of light on something—this time, a dancing frog that had cost a quarter—that would, for all intents and purposes, disappear after she pushed a button. A corollary emerged. The more methodical the thinking behind Shirley's invention, the more specifically it could mete out destruction.

Some improvements to the potato launcher came from unforeseen shortages in materials. One day, the two had run out of hairspray. In a pinch, Shirley visited the medicine cabinet and started reading labels. She came across a brown can of Right Guard and was amazed to find that it had three different volatile propellants. There were almost six lines of caution, printed in small type, warning about its flammability, which was a good sign. Conducting a simple test with a lighter, Shirley knew she had a winner. She felt the heat on her face as an impressive flame jumped out with a roar. The flame was much larger and hotter than what hairspray had netted.

Shirley wondered how in the heck such a turbo-charged, clean-burning mixture of fuels had been specially designed for battling armpit stink. Regardless, she was happy that it did.

Field tests concluded that Right Guard was the clear and easy winner. More loudly and noticeably faster, potatoes launched across the rural landscape.

As per spraying the stuff in armpits, it also dried mostly on contact. There was less gumminess to clear out of the chamber after long afternoons spent firing.

It was during this period of quick-moving advancements that Shirley became distracted in the field. Sitting on the tailgate of her station wagon, Shirley was debating with herself if she should make and bring along a little wind meter. Wind was one of the elements working against a fully predictable potato launch. She was listening to Rachel with only half an ear when her granddaughter asked her a question.

"Grandma, it didn't fire. Any ideas?"

Shirley, not paying attention to her granddaughter, stuck her finger in her mouth, then held it aloft. She felt a slight breeze against it. It was obvious to Rachel that her question didn't register.

"Grandma, what should I do?"

Shirley's eyes flicked over to her granddaughter, but her mind was on a different carousel, one that included miniature spinning cups catching the wind.

"Grandma?"

Still nothing from Shirley. She picked up a handful of dirt and watched it fall. The finer dust fell away at an angle, along with the slight breeze, while rocks fell straight down.

Rachel, having launched potatoes successfully hundreds of times, but never having a misfire, took her grandma's lack of response to take it upon herself to figure out the problem herself. She was almost an adult. Rachel unscrewed the endcap of the launcher, peered inside, and clicked the trigger to see if there was a spark, knowing that two things make an explosion: fuel and fire. The unexpected answer to Rachel's scientific inquiry was a fireball that leapt out of the chamber, instantly burning off the part of her eyebrows that extended above her safety glasses. Alarmed and frightened, Rachel's head whipped back as she patted out her on-fire bangs. Her entire face was hot and red.

Shirley jolted as the fireball engulfed Rachel's head. In that instant, she swore she saw all the way through the face flesh to her granddaughter's skull and it terrified her. She bolted towards her granddaughter. "Rache, oh, Rache," Shirley pleaded. "Are you okay? Baby girl, are you okay?"

Smoke eerily rose from Rachel's forehead as she removed her hands from her face. "How do I look?"

Shirley quickly scrutinized her granddaughter's face. Luckily, with little exception, it looked like she'd just gotten a sunburn. Rachel began shaking as Shirley delicately touched her granddaughter's face. "Oh, Rache. I think you're okay. Just real red. Can you take off the glasses?" Rachel had a racooney look, like a tourist who'd fallen asleep in the sun with their sunglasses on. "Thank goodness you had those on." She stroked Rachel's face, smoothed out what was left of her eyebrows, and tapped out the last burning patch of hair. "Honey, I think you're going to be okay. Okay?"

Rachel started crying, and not from physical hurt but from fright.

"Oh, it's okay." Shirley patted Rachel's back as she hugged her tight. "It's okay."

"You're not mad?"

"Mad? Why would I be mad?"

"Me being stupid. Me wrecking your gun."

"Don't be silly. Tell me what happened."

"The launcher didn't fire, so I took the cap off and clicked the ignition."

Shirley knew that the latent gases were volatile for a good ten minutes—especially with that Right Guard—that a bit too healthy of a squirt could make the fuel mixture too rich. All of that didn't mean a lick if her granddaughter got hurt. "Rache, that's not too good of an idea. Promise not to do it again? Just wait awhile." Shirley blamed herself for thinking about wind and not paying attention.

Rachel cried into her grandmother's shoulder and answered with a whimpering "Yeah, I was stupid."

The launcher lay on the ground, unscathed.

"We just have to be really, really careful all the time," Shirley whispered. "You and me both. Okay?"

"Okay."

"Promise?"

"Yeah."

"You're probably going to have to use a little extra eyebrow pencil until it grows back in."

Rachel laughed, choked on a bubble of spit, and laughed again.

Then they both cried softly, feeling so close to a large, steep emotional ledge.

"Let's call it a day. I'll pack up. You just sit down."

Rachel sat in the passenger seat, flipped down the visor, and studied herself in the vanity mirror. "Fuckin' awesome," she whispered to herself as she punched the bench seat. "It looks like I've got a fake tan." She vacantly fingered the ridge where her eyebrows used to be.

CHAPTER TWENTY-ONE
Hiding in Plain View

Shirley and Rachel were stopped at a train crossing; the station wagon buffeted by the wind generated by a roaring train. The metronomic clanging of a warning signal was out of synch with the flashing lights. One second, Shirley was thinking about her daughter's eyebrows and what color of pencil would work best to fill them in so they'd look somewhat natural, and the very next moment, she found herself reliving the day she decided to turn her wardrobe day-glo.

Her father, Konrad, loved bow hunting and young Shirley had often seen the prey. Although she didn't have a taste for killing, she admired her father's respect of the animals he hunted. No part was wasted. There was no boasting. Clean kill shots. Her father learned how to hunt from necessity in Poland when his father's farm had been razed and the only animals left to eat were wild. Wanda, Shirley's mother, was a quiet participant and an amateur naturalist. She enjoyed watching pretty things and thought the antics of squirrels were hilarious.

Many times, Shirley had witnessed a deer lying on the forest floor, as if in rest, but with a stick poking out of its fur, bright feathers at the end: an arrow piercing the deer's heart. Most often, there was little, if any, blood. The deer often looked like it was just taking a nap on a bed of leaves, and not in its final rest, that it would shake the arrow out of its shank and bound away. Konrad was a big man, but if the deer was larger, he'd fashion a drag-along from branches and pull the animal behind him. It was Shirley's duty to carry the bow back to the truck.

Hours would go in silence and stillness, and there were periods when Shirley, Konrad, and Wanda would feel nature relax around them, like curtains opening to a play that was up to a receptive audience to appreciate. Shirley loved sitting and observing without feeling she was being watched by anything with a brain and that could talk. Birds chirped and serenity cloaked them.

The trio would often sit apart from one another, blending into the scenery, all three camouflaged.

For such a predictable equation that a day of hunting had become, one day something didn't make sense.

Shirley's mother stood straight up, stock still, her left hand outstretched, looking like she was checking the pulse of the tree, like it was a friend's neck. Her mother didn't make a sound and Shirley had to really concentrate over the hundred yards of forest that separated them—"Why does Mom keep touching that tree?"

A dark stream of red fluid started to stain the bark of the tree.

A rustle of movement a hundred yards away to Shirley's left, and Shirley's father, expertly camouflaged as a lump of earth, stood up, empty bow in hand.

Konrad moved like the animals he hunted: low to the earth, hunched to not give away his six feet of height, padding softly, weaving within the paths between the shrubs so as to not snap their branches. He knelt down to what he'd been aiming at and cursed in a whisper.

The deer had unexpectedly flinched the moment he had released the arrow. Instead of painlessly killing the animal by stopping its heart between beats, the arrow had gone through the front of its skull, in one eye socket and out the other. On the ground, near the deer's twitching body was an eyeball, sliced in half by the arrow's flight, the iris itself, split.

Konrad quietly cursed again when he realized that the arrow was neither in or near the body, unsheathed a knife, cupped the deer's head in one hand, and slit its throat—deeply, swiftly—with the other.

It was not the way he'd wished it.

Also like an animal, Konrad felt that something around him was wrong. He stood up slowly and turned. And then he saw his wife, Wanda, not far from where he knew she was hiding, checking the pulse of a tree.

"It was my fault," Wanda said in a soft voice that carried but did not reach Konrad's ears.

Konrad had much keener eyesight than his daughter and immediately began to run towards his wife. The bright feathers at the end of the arrow, to him, as plain as a roadside flare.

"It was my fault," Wanda repeated as Konrad took secret pride that his wife wasn't screaming, or even crying, although an arrow had pierced her hand and had impaled it to an oak.

He looked into his wife's eyes, which were steely and defiant and much different than the soft gaze of a deer. Konrad quickly accessed the situation. Shirley, somewhat paralyzed until that moment, popped up from hiding and ran towards her parents.

"This will hurt," Konrad said as he slipped his hand between Wanda's and the tree trunk. He firmly pulled his wife's hand way from the trunk along the shaft of the arrow, which became lubricated with blood, so he could establish a firm grip. From a pocket, Konrad produced a multiple utility tool that he had made himself, flashed it open and locked heavy duty scissors into place. He cut the end off the arrow, dropped the tool, pried his wife's hand from the shaft, and whipped out a clean handkerchief in one fluid motion.

"I'd never seen one before," Wanda said as Konrad wrapped her hand tightly, providing the pressure to stop the bleeding. "Its wings were so blue, like they were made out of stained glass."

Calm returned to Konrad. His wife was not going to die. "A butterfly?" he asked.

Shirley reached her parents, huffing, her side aching from running so quickly.

"Is that why you moved?" Konrad asked, unbuttoning Wanda's shirtsleeve. With one hand, he pushed the fabric back. Using his index and middle fingers, he checked her pulse.

"I'm sorry," Wanda said. Her voice was tinted with disappointment in herself. She knew better than to move suddenly. She was a safe woman. The butterfly had looked like a fluttering jewel.

Konrad began to laugh. At first, it was a nervous laugh that helped push back the pain of shooting his wife. Then it was a hearty laugh because he hadn't killed her, and the laughing looked like it felt so good, that—although she was in quite a bit of pain—Wanda began laughing. It was the loudest noise Shirley ever remembered while being in the forest. Laughter echoed off of valley walls, bouncing back warbly and full of echo.

Her parents hugged so tightly that all Shirley could do was wrap herself tightly around her father's legs. She looked at the tip of the arrow, with its nub of shaft, bloody, in the tree trunk, and all she could think of was how she could avoid getting shot, even by accident, even by someone who undoubtedly loved her.

And what she thought was so clear and so big in her mind that it was like a herd of elephants rushing towards her. The impression that day left was deep, like the footprints of elephants in mud. The two thoughts were these: make yourself so obvious that you don't get trampled. Make yourself so obvious so you're never mistaken for a target.

That very night, years and years and years ago, little Shirley began knitting her first bright yellow sweater. She wore it the next time they all went hunting. Soon after, she took to wearing bright clothing every day.

From that day on, Shirley insisted on hiding in plain view.

"Hey Grandma," Rachel gently poked her mother's arm.

Shirley stared, glassy eyed, ahead of her, into an open landscape.

"The train's gone. We can go now."

And with that, not turning towards her daughter, Shirley quickly glanced at the back of her left hand—which was free from scarring, unlike her mother's—took off the parking brake, put the car into drive, and pushed down on the gas.

CHAPTER TWENTY-TWO
The New Button

Shirley found herself openly questioning how everyday things worked. "Just how does a car suck in its fuel?" she asked as she was at a stop sign. She put her car in neutral, gunned the gas, and listened attentively until the car behind her honked its horn in three quick, cheery bleats. Shirley waved in her rearview mirror and continued through the intersection. When Shirley got home from work, she went inside, snapped on some rubber gloves, popped the hood, and stood in front of her car. Hood up, she revved the engine by flicking the fuel throttle arm on the side of the carburetor. Air filter removed and off to the side, she tilted her head sideways to see the action of the gasoline being sucked into engine to be ignited. With a flashlight, she saw that the gasoline was being atomized. "A relatively consistent explosive environment," Shirley muttered in a voice that triggered her memory to write that down. "That's what the car depends on to run smoothly."

At work, Shirley breached a topic with one of the computer techs.

"So, the little fans in the computers," Shirley began.

"The CPU fan?"

"I think. The one I can hear right now."

"The CPU fan."

"Does it produce a spark?"

The tech guy wasn't expecting that question. "Some of them don't. They're called brushless."

"Do they cost much?" Shirley asked.

"Yours sounds fine. They make a lot of noise before they die. Kinda like a screeching cat."

"No, for my granddaughter's computer at home. I'm not asking for one. I just need to know what to buy."

The tech guy looked at Rachel's framed portrait on Shirley's desk, couldn't quite put together why Shirley was concerned about sparks, ultimately decided he didn't care, but that he wouldn't mind seeing Shirley's granddaughter in the flesh. The makeup made Rachel look older. "I'll see what I can do."

"Oh, I wasn't expecting one. I can go get it myself," Shirley said, pencil at the ready over a sticky note. "Can you just tell me a model number and size?"

"She a punk rocker?" the tech guy asked.

Shirley looked up to the tech guy and followed his gaze a foot over to the left on her desk. "She really likes a band… I can't remember their name, but they sing about lobotomies and sniffing glue."

"Can't go wrong with the Ramones." The tech guy smiled. He knew he probably had more in common with the girl in the frame than most of the people he worked with. "Don't sweat it. We may have some in surplus." He leaned in closer, conspiratorially, "Some of your bosses, they just upgrade to upgrade. We've got extras that are used, but work fine."

A few hours later, two CPU fans in a plain white paper bag showed up on Shirley's desk. Inside was a note, messily written. "These won't spark. The size is 50mm. Let me know if you have any more questions." He hadn't signed the note, which slightly bothered Shirley.

That evening, with full eye protection and a fire extinguisher within reach, Shirley carefully pinched a fan into a vice clamp.

She had figured out a way to wire the fan by making a switch and hooking it up to a single nine-volt battery. The fan whirred. She sprayed it with Right Guard. It continued to whir, a little wetter. Shirley honked a five-second spray into the guts of the fan. It continued whirring. No sparks. No uncontrollable fire. No fan malfunction. Shirley pressed another healthy squirt into the fan, then lit the fumes on fire for a brief second. The fan continued to whir.

It only took a couple of evenings for Shirley to fully install and mount the computer fan in the rear of the chamber. She made a stable bracket out of a single piece of tin that she cut, reshaped, drilled, and folded. Push a button, the fan whirred. Take a finger off, it stopped. A switch is the simplest thing in the world, yet it gave Shirley joy that it worked as designed.

Shirley intentionally wouldn't tell Rachel about her advancements before unveiling them in the field. She wanted to see how attentive Rachel was. Rachel was one of the few who could see through the mirror that her grandma held up to the world because she, too, did the exact same thing.

"I see we've got a new button," Rachel observed.

"Yeah," Shirley said evasively as she took the gun out of its brown and orange zigzagged knitted sheath. "Want to help me set some stuff up?" Out of a large blue tub, Shirley pulled out a pink elephant, its trunk broken, where it had once held a light aloft. "Watch out for the cord; it's still attached. Got it for a steal. Fifty cents."

Rachel touched the white, jagged, broken-off nub. "People really buy this stuff new, don't they?"

"Someone has to," Shirley said vacantly.

The women set up a menagerie of lawn figurines, many with wide grins or purposeful gestures. The diorama of damaged goods looked like a cartoon, its characters unaware that they were about to walk through the valley of death.

Shirley loaded up a spud in the barrel. "I've got big hopes

for this little fan." She unscrewed the back of the fuel chamber. "So, I'm squirting Right Guard into the back," which she did. "Then, I screw it back on and turn on the fan by pushing this button."

"I can barely hear it," Rachel reported.

"That little guy, I believe, is going to mix the fuel with the air inside the chamber evenly. No longer will part of the chamber be starved and another too rich. It's like a carburetor. My hope is that it'll improve reliability—no more misfiring—and put a little more oomph in the muzzle velocity department as an added bonus." Shirley took her finger off the fan and motioned Rachel to don the rifle muffs over her ears. She did the same. "Better move back a bit."

By this time, Shirley's legs had become considerably more powerful than when she'd begun with the slingshot. She'd also become a better marksman. Being another gray day, the laser pointer's red line shone right between the grinning elephant's eyes. Shirley twisted her feet into the gravel for more grip, then pulled the trigger.

Several things happened almost simultaneously: the rifle roared louder than ever before; a potato was launched just a hair short of the sound barrier; a smiling elephant lost its entire head and half of its torso; and Shirley, although fully braced, staggered a step back, her hands tingling from the jolt.

A plaster mist settled and nothing above the elephant's pink belly button came back into sight. Keeping the muzzle pointed down range, Shirley turned to her granddaughter and said, "I think my data was correct."

"God damn right it was!" Rachel whooped.

Shirley shook her head in disbelief at her own creation, then turned around and jotted some numbers down on a clipboard. The numbers were above what she had calculated. Then she looked up at Rachel. "I know you're excited, but I wish you wouldn't swear so much."

"Sorry, grandma. I'm just so happy for you."

Shirley let it slide. "Now, I just hit the fan again." Shirley paused for dramatic effect as the fan blew a noticeable, lazy wisp of spent fuel through the barrel. It looked like a giant, white cigar. "And it ventilates itself. Don't have to worry about any latent fumes."

"Want to give it a try? Just make sure you really lean into it." Rachel was lean, lithe, full of hidden muscles, and had no trouble shooting the launcher.

One by one, all of the animals vanished into vapor. It looked like a mini blizzard had touched down on a twenty-foot piece of land. There was literally nothing they could clean up unless they had a vacuum cleaner.

"Well, I think that's all I'm going to do with this one," Shirley said as she unscrewed the endcap, scooped out potato remnants, then inspected the gun for any signs of stress. "Any more power and the PVC will start to degrade and fail. All it needs now is a paint job. Would you do the honors?"

Rachel bowed down before her grandmother, much how she imagined a knight would do in front of a queen. Although overacting, she was sincere. "Yes, m'lady. As long as you don't mind pink."

The next day, after Shirley had masked off the wire, trigger, and vulnerable parts, the gun was painted a bright, bright pink, like a bottle of Pepto Bismol had been poured all over it. Rachel painted an eagle on the thickest part of the chamber, in a deeper shade of pink. Shirley thought it looked like the bird on the dollar bill. Rachel painted it in homage to Joey, Dee Dee, Tommy, and Johnny Ramone, members of one of the best damn bands. Ever.

CHAPTER TWENTY-THREE
Electrocution by a Rare Form of Happiness

Months passed. Thousands of potatoes destroyed unfortunate figurines abandoned for pennies on the dollar at garage sales. Both women's marksmanship rivaled those of the Sussex County Sheriff.

With each successive launch, Shirley became more and more confident that she could dispatch something larger—around fifteen pounds—and she could launch it just as hard and just as straight. She saw potatoes as smaller pumpkins, and with every potato exploded, the nuances of the explosive characteristics of underarm deodorant, potato mass, gravity, and friction became clearer and clearer. For Shirley, each test was like watching someone paint a large mural. First are the large background strokes, then the slightly smaller areas in a different color that separate the main parts, and finally, with the smallest brush and delicate strokes, the entire painting reveals itself in razor-sharp detail, both massive and precise.

The ballistic difference between an eight-ounce potato and a fifteen-pound pumpkin was immense. If the spud gun had been a waltz with Sir Isaac Newton, the first several months of planning for the pumpkin was like a pogo, a dance Shirley had just recently come in contact with a second time. As she was passing Rachel's door, she heard thumping on the ground. After her knocks went unanswered, she edged the door open, to see Rachel in mid-jump, arm's flailing to the beat like a jump rope, fingers snapping. A cord attached Rachel's headphones to her stereo. Rachel didn't hear her grandma come in, but became embarrassed when she saw her standing near the door. Rachel slid the headphones down to her neck. The music blasted quietly across the room as Rachel's air guitar quickly disappeared from her fingers.

"What are you doing?" Shirley asked.

"I'm dancing," Rachel replied, sheepishly.

"I can see that. What's the dance called?"

"Pogo."

"Like, as in pogo stick?"

"I guess that's where it came from. Never thought about it."

"Is it popular at school?"

"I don't think so. I'm not too sure what dance is popular at school. Not a lot of kids are dancing in the hallways."

"So, it's like this?" Shirley tentatively jumped up and down a couple of times, then really started to go for it, almost losing her balance. "That's all?" she asked, slightly winded from the unexpected activity.

"Pretty much." Rachel didn't know how she felt about her grandma working on dance moves, or that her grandma considered pogoing "dancing" and not just getting into music. At first, she hoped that she could keep some things for herself, but immediately softened as she watched Shirley jump up and down. She looked like a prairie dog popping in and out of a hole. Shirley had a way of making potentially menacing activities seem as dangerous as baking a fresh batch of brownies.

"I just like doing it, grandma. It fits the music. It's a good way to release some energy."

"Not a bad workout, either," Shirley huffed. "I knocked before coming in."

"It's okay."

From where Shirley was standing across the room, the

sound emanating out from around her granddaughter's neck was like animals screaming as traffic hit them. She didn't quite understand how Rachel could like it so much. What was wrong with a little harmony, a little melody? Mel Torme. The Limeliters. The Kingston Trio. Were they so bad?

Shirley shut her granddaughter's door and Rachel continued her appreciation of a compilation tape a friend had just made her. One song from the Bags ended as another song from the Cheifs blasted through the tiny speakers on the headphones. The songs affected her body, like she was being electrocuted by a rare form of happiness.

CHAPTER TWENTY-FOUR
Equations' Tendons

Shirley's confidence in her new plan was being hammered against an anvil of doubt, despite her success with the potato gun. In the end, this hammering would make her invention all the more sharp and resilient. Yet, in the beginning stages of preparation, her mind couldn't keep up with all of the elements she had to corral that were jumping all around her like heated popcorn kernels in a pan with no lid. Mentally, her feet barely seem to hit the ground. She always seemed on the verge of losing her breath. At first, she wanted to use the material she had already become intimate with—PVC—but became more and more convinced that it wouldn't be able to take the pressure. It was like knitting the pouch for the slingshot. What's a great idea for one activity can prove dismal for another. She didn't want to go off killing herself or Rachel. The exploding catapult haunted her. She even found herself involuntarily shuddering when scanning the channels and championship bowling was on TV. The clacking and crunching sounds of the balls whacking pins terrified her. She also wanted to ditch using flammable propellants. Her granddaughter should be reasonably free of the danger of losing her eyebrows again in the name of science. Question marks took the place of sure strokes in her physics journal.

"These aren't wrinkles to refine," Shirley muttered to herself.

"This won't be a variation of the same beast. It's a different species. A new breed." She clutched a pencil so hard that it took a couple seconds of her fingers stinging for her to realize that she'd snapped it in half. Shirley pushed back from her desk, grabbed her coat, and took a long walk.

All the different components of the experiment lashed at her. It was like an octopus in the sky—tentacles whipping at her from eight different directions, its suction cups puckering, but she couldn't see how they were all connected at the source. It didn't fall together. She didn't want to make a pumpkin-launching cannon that would just explode. She didn't want a limp-projectile cannon. The desire to strike back in one decisive action was growing and growing. "No," she said as she rounded the last corner back to her house. "It doesn't make sense." She intentionally put more weight on her left leg and felt it buckle ever so slightly as a reminder to the promise she'd made for herself. Then she rubbed her left forearm. She hadn't sufficiently punched the world back in the arm. Not quite yet.

Shirley imagined a fancy ballroom where a phalanx of the great physicists, inventors, and scientists got together and danced. They provided footy diagrams, and instead of the Foxtrot or Jitterbug, they danced using involved equations from gyroscopic motion to the graceful arc of gravitational pull.

It helped Shirley comprehend how all of the elements converged. Galileo Galilee and his force of gravity tangoed with Newton, that sexy rascal who shimmy shimmy shaked out his equations of motion. Heinrich Gustav Magnus' fleet-footed ruminations of downward directed force cha-cha-cha'd with Benoulli's correlations of higher streaming velocities. Physics. Ballistics. History. All were big dances in and of themselves. All together, they were a demolition derby in her brain.

Shirley was overwhelmed.

Her diagrams were chaotic, incomplete. But the ends of them weren't broken. They were sticky. They were like bits of gum, waiting on a hot sidewalk, ready to be stepped upon and scraped off onto another place. These incomplete ideas were merely tendons awaiting to be attached to bones.

"Yes," Shirley muttered at all the black holes in her diagrams, "it is just a pumpkin launcher in a town that hardly anyone would miss if it were permanently erased from every map in the world." She thickly scribbled out a line of symbols with her pencil, so its tip became blunt. "But it's going to be the most accurate, forceful pumpkin launcher."

Shirley's nerves calmed considerably as she came across Rudolf Clausius' second law of thermodynamics. The entropy of the universe always increases. Chaos is at the edge of all classical mechanics. Everything was going according to a larger plan. Problem was, the unifying plan wasn't making any kind of sense. And she hadn't even gotten to the step where she acquired one single piece of material for the pumpkin launcher.

"Want to go on a bike ride?" Shirley asked Rachel. Ever since Shirley had started her garage sale walking regimen, her body craved motion. Movement proved to be the best medicine for her. It also seemed that repeated motions activated a different part of her brain that had been securely locked for a long, long time.

"Sure," Rachel said, looking up, and sliding a bookmark into place, removing a whip of strawberry licorice, which she'd been using as a straw in a pop can, then biting it.

The two biked around for awhile, meandering over the mostly empty streets, careful not to hit the solid chunks of ice that had been plowed to the side and had become cement-hard from melting slightly in the day and re-freezing at night.

As they reached the top of a small, rolling peak, Shirley pulled a water from the bicycle's bottle cage and offered it to Rachel. It was ice cold. They felt it thread through their chests as they swallowed it down.

"So, grandma, what's on your mind?"

Shirley wasn't quite sure. There were so many physicists still dancing in her mind. The song was continuous. There were no breaks in the orchestral movements. She didn't want to sound crazy.

"You seem distracted," Rachel continued, after her grandma offered a mild nod in response.

"Rache," Shirley started, "I'm just thinking. That's all. Trying to wrap my brain around the cannon. I just can't make a bigger potato gun."

"I know that, but I'm kind of worried about you."

"Don't be, honey. I'm just thinking."

"Well, what about, exactly? Maybe I can help you out," Rachel offered.

There was another pause as a slight wind began cooling them down, their sweat beginning to evaporate.

"Have you ever heard of Maupertuis?"

"I take it that he's a physicist."

"Something like that. An all-around thinker. French guy born over three hundred years ago, who a lot of folks didn't take too seriously because he tried to come up with silly stuff like a calculus of pain and pleasure. Because he was kind of off, other people came along, developed his un-nutty theories, and got credit for them." Shirley's foot tapped one of her pedals. It spun around and around. "He came up with idea of the Principle of Least Action."

"I could get into that," Rachel encouraged.

"He supposed that the perfection of the universe as a whole demands that it be efficient and concise. Spare. No motions are wasted."

Rachel had no idea how what her grandma was talking about had any correlation to launching pumpkins, but she nodded just the same.

"Natural motions—like riding a bike—can be done with a certain economy. It doesn't help if you wave your arms around when you're pedaling. Or if you're going down a hill, after a certain point, it's better just to coast along instead of pedaling really fast. So, it's not being lazy. It's not working more than you have to. You're working on not wasting energy. I'm trying to think around adding gadgets to the machine that I won't need in the end. What I'm looking for is the most direct path to put a whole bunch of pressure behind a pumpkin so it'll fly really fast but it won't turn into pumpkin pie right from the barrel, right?"

Rachel nodded.

"Well, I think I'm on to something. I don't think I can jinx it, because I don't exactly know what it is. You know how…" Shirley's voice traveled off.

"It's okay. Let's have it," Rachel coaxed.

"I think that the little things we can't see when we launch potatoes are the key to the pumpkin. Small things, things I can't write down in my notebook yet—or ever—those may be the most important things to understand."

"But you can't see them. How are you going to see them?" There was an edge to Rachel's voice that she didn't expect. She wanted to be supportive. She was getting cold. "Are you talking about a microscope?"

"No… maybe. Not quite, but that's the spirit of what I'm trying to get at." Shirley clopped her mitts together. She grimaced, then smiled through gritted teeth. "That's what I'm betting on, though. It's the little things before the pumpkin's loaded that'll affect everything. That's why I'm in no hurry to start building. All the pieces have to fit conceptually. There are always those one or two potatoes that veer way off course when we go shooting. I think that's more a product of the design than an oddly shaped potato."

"Is that why you haven't made anything yet?"

"I think… I think…" Shirley's mind coasted. Words weren't coming easily. "Potatoes aren't perfect bullets. They're irregular. Pumpkins will be, too. So, when we launch them, it gives the impression that the outcome is random. I don't think so. I think that if I make a simple, powerful machine that's very sensitive to a lot of details we can't really see but are all around us… it'll blow… I think I could blow a pumpkin right through a car."

"From how far away?" Rachel had become somewhat desensitized to vegetables vaporizing solid objects, but a car was definitely progress.

"I'm willing to guess 400 yards." Shirley continued gritting her teeth. She knew it was all conjecture. The more she talked about it, the more she felt like she was brushing herself into a self-portrait of failure.

"Really? That far?"

"I'm hoping so."

"All the way through a car?"

"Yes."

"Grandma, don't let it bum you out."

"I'm not bummed," Shirley replied. "As I said before, I'm just thinking about it." With that, she put a foot back on her pedal. "It's getting cold." Puffs of white air confirmed it. "Let's go home and make some apple cider."

A half an hour later, hands warmed by mugs, feet warmed by a fire, Shirley felt a little more comfortable about what she'd already said and wanted to continue. "So, Newton…"

"You really like-like that guy, don't you?"

Shirley tried to suppress a blush but failed. "With his mind. He was really a troubled man who had a couple of nervous breakdowns, which I'd like to avoid. Newton's theory of gravitation provides a simple solution to the problem of two mutually attracting bodies."

Rachel raised an eyebrow at the words "attracting bodies."

Shirley didn't blush this time. She was already in a trough of thought. "For example, take the sun and any planet in the solar system. Right? With Newton's equations and observations, astronomers can predict how, say, Venus will revolve around the sun. The sun's so big. Its gravitational pull is huge. We know how two bodies interact, but physicists still don't really know how—if there's a third planet plopped into the equation—how to predict all three will affect one another."

"But our solar system already has more than two planets," Rachel contended.

"The sun's so big. All the planets' individual gravitational pulls are nothing compared to it. That's why Newton's model works so well—it's just the relation of planets to the sun. Physicists still can't predict what will exactly happen when two of the smaller planets get close enough to have a gravitational effect on one another while simultaneously getting pulled on by the sun." The three-body problem is mathematically unsolvable. When two smaller planets are close enough in our solar system, how they move is called an 'aberration'."

"I don't quite get what that has to do with launching pumpkins." Rachel said. "We're only launching one pumpkin at a time."

"Nothing, really. It's just that nobody can prove the three-body problem. It's very possible that the solar system's unstable. What we can't figure out—the gravitational attractions between the planets themselves—may lead to one of those planets plooping off into outer space." Shirley shrugged. "It just makes me feel small. But it's also freeing. There's so much more figuring out to do for all of us." Shirley finally sipped her cider. She placed the cup down. Her words formed, like pieces of popcorn being slowly needled onto a string. "I just don't want to fail. I guess that's it. There are so many things to think of. It's hard to figure out what's important."

In a lull one day, Shirley had pulled down the newspaper article of the first annual pumpkin chuck, fragile with age and lightly speckled with paint, and placed it on the workbench. Shirley was mildly surprised that the article had yellowed so much. Time was passing fast. Feeling archival, not wanting the article to completely disintegrate, she proceeded to cover it with strip after strip of clear packing tape, laminating both its front and back. She used a pin to take the air out of small bubbles that had formed during the process, smoothing them all out. Still pliable enough to fold, it felt like an ancient map to a treasure she knew could be hers if she could be keen and tenacious enough to decipher all its clues.

Shirley surprised herself even more when she started talking to the picture of the plaster trophy with the leprechaun holding the pumpkin aloft.

"You're mine, little man. You hear me? I'm taking you home and strapping you to my roof."

With no one else around, it didn't quite feel like boasting. It felt more like self-affirmation.

Her finger was pointed stiffly at the tiny man with an orange beard, pipe clenched in his mouth, struggling beneath the plaster pumpkin. "You're coming home with momma."

Being a rank amateur at trash talking, Shirley quickly ran out of things to say and just stood there, eyes fixed and smoldering, pointing her finger at the photograph, shaking it with small trembles, until she started laughing at herself.

"But dang it, I *do* really want it," Shirley said. This ambition made her feel like she had swallowed a fireball and it was burning her up inside.

She looked down at the newspaper clipping again. "You're coming with me." She folded it back and forth several times, over multiple seams, until it was collapsible and flat. She then slid it in her pocket and patted it down. "You're mine."

Every day after, from that day forward until she completed her mission, after waking up and completing her morning rituals, directly after she clasped on her watch, she made sure she had the newspaper clipping in her front pocket.

CHAPTER TWENTY-FIVE
No. I Like Laughing.

The dance continued in Shirley's mind, and one day, about six months later, all of the scientists cleared the floor and the dry, scraping footprints of their theories quieted. She wasn't quite ready for an ending. It just came. There was nothing else to pre-figure out. An entire machine—from theoretical concept to actual blueprint—filled her notebook. It was all there. She was sure of it. No gaping holes.

"I'll be danged," Shirley whispered in disbelief. "That looks like it'll work." She flipped through the pages, one by one, her disbelief growing with each page. "It's bigger than I thought."

It was going to be extremely difficult to build. It had to be. Otherwise every half-wit goofball would have a pumpkin launcher, knocking out their neighbors' windows. It'd be anarchy.

Chet's skepticism of Shirley had softened somewhat, mainly due to the fact that she had never returned any of the haphazard parts she'd purchased. Nonetheless, he positioned himself out of sight, behind the key-making machine for several minutes before strolling out into the aisles.

Shirley was holding a bright yellow rubber ball with both hands, looking at welding equipment.

Chet's confidence slumped once again, his smile a cheap paper mask. "How may I help you today, ma'am?"

Shirley held up the ball. "I need a length of pipe, aluminum, that this ball will slide into."

"Ooh, we're not going to have it, I can tell you that. Too big."

"Do you know where I can get one?"

"Not too sure. I'd start by looking in the phone book."

The building was single story, industrial. It was painted a nondescript tan and, like all of the buildings surrounding it, covered in a silt of dust and metal shavings. The air was acrid, smelling vaguely of a semi's over-used brakes going down a steep decline. Shirley knew she was at the right place when she read "Stoobs' Machining" painted above the doorway. She knocked on the door. No one answered. She knocked some more, noticing that the door gave a little as her knuckles rapped the metal frame. She pushed the door open and knocked on the dust-blanketed desk immediately inside the door. "Hello? Mr. Stoobs?"

"Whum en."

"Mr. Stoobs?"

"Wes!"

Shirley rounded the corner that separated the small office from the main work area. A man with shockingly white, short, and erect hair looked at her, his mouth full of Vienna sausages. Placing the tin down, he chewed quickly and cleared his throat. His hands were filthy, the tops of his fingernails crescents of dark moons. He was using a plastic fork to harpoon the mini canned meats. "Yes? May I help you?" For a brief second, Stoobs thought the woman was lost. She wore a broach of a knitted cat over her breast. She was carrying a bright yellow ball. Not his typical customer.

"Mr. Stoobs?"

"Yes... You caught me during lunch."

"I'm sorry. I can wait."

"No, no." Stoobs pushed the lid of the can back down, pin-

133

ning the fork, and covering the remaining sausages, which bobbed in their juice. He swallowed the last remnants of sausage down with some cold coffee. "What can I do for you?" He bounced off of his high-seated chair onto the floor. He seemed to be made of high-tension springs, coiled tightly. Not a large man, but a man whose muscles were in constant use, forcing metal into new, precise shapes. It was a body that had become, in many ways, the human equivalent to his machines.

Shirley didn't know it, but Stoobs was a man who could resurrect the dead. Car repair shops in a hundred-mile radius knew that if a part was no longer available—wasn't made or couldn't be found in a junkyard—that Stoobs could fabricate it. All he needed was the dimensions and the material it was to be made of. That was why Stoobs never answered his phone. Why? Business always came to him, on his time.

"Can you do any specialty rifling?" Shirley asked.
"What do you have in mind?"

"Promise not to laugh?"

"No. I like laughing. What do you have in mind?"

"Can you rifle a ten inch barrel?"

"You mean a ten-inch long barrel?"

"No, a ten inch-diameter barrel. One that a ball like this would fit in." Shirley raised the ball in her palms.

"A cannon barrel?"

"You could say that," Shirley reiterated.

"That's what I'm saying, ma'am. A cannon barrel?"

"Yes."

"What's it for?"

"Pumpkins."

"What did pumpkins ever do to you?"

"Nothing. Why?"

"Why do you want to shoot 'em?"

"Just to see if I can do it."

The logic was infallible to Stoobs. He scratched his chin. He, too, had blown up many things for no better reason than to see what would happen. The gears in his clock-like brain began clicking. Sprockets meshed, teeth clacked together, springs activated. "You're not gonna shoot down planes with it, are you?" Stoobs had already ruled out the possibility that Shirley was a Civil War reenactor. Shirley was wearing one of her self-knit sweaters. It was bright yellow and matched the ball. From the contrast, it made the brown cat broach literally jump off her chest.

"You're not going to be loading bowling balls in this and taking out a bank, are you?" Stoobs asked, not that he really cared, he just wanted to be free of potential liabilities. He regarded the woman standing in front of him less dangerous than the plastic fork he was using moments before.

"I'll be crushed if I hit a bird by accident," Shirley replied.

"'Cause I don't want to be no accomplice. Pumpkins, you say?"

"Pumpkins."

"Why ten inch diameter?"

"That's the regulations," Shirley replied.

"You mean this is a competition?"

"Yes," Shirley answered meekly.

"Shit, ma'am, I did much stupider stuff when I was a kid," Stoobs said as he walked over to a light switch and flicked it on. "Ever stick a lizard in a jar, fill it up with gas, plug it with a cloth as a wick, light it, then throw it into traffic?"

Shirley blinked, and thought. "No, can't say that I have."

Stoobs studied Shirley. She wasn't reviled. She could take a joke. He was beginning to like her. "The lizards smell something awful, like burnt ribs and the smell penetrates, travels like skunk scent."

Fluorescent lights hummed to life, illuminating an incredible amount of machines for such a confined space. They were like metal cattle, all penned up, patiently waiting on an uncertain future. Stoobs wove expertly through them, his mind already working a spiral through metal, remembering that the sine wave was a good default for rifling a barrel.

"How'd you hear about me?" Stoobs asked as he clanked large metal plates aside and looked into the belly of one of his machines.

"The yellow pages."

"I'm still listed? I stopped paying them yahoos years ago. Motherfuckers kept on calling me, wanting me to advertise. Crap." There was a loud clank. Stoobs looked up in Shirley's direction. "Pardon. After seeing so many men die, it's hard to care about my language."

"You're close to my house. I live a couple miles away. You're the first machinist I've visited."

Stoobs quietly burped into his hands. He really liked sausages, even their smells after he'd eaten them. "That so?"

Shirley nodded. "Yep."

"I'm kind of hard to find. I like you, though. Not many women come through my doors." Stoobs banged deeper into hidden shelves of dies and casts, lathe parts, disks, fittings, and rods. "Well, shit me a canoe." Stoobs lugged a large, heavy piece of metal to his workbench, pulled out a caliper, measured, looked at Shirley, and said, "I do believe we're in business." Stoobs' lips pursed as he figured how he was going to center and mount the cutter on an industrial lathe, which weighed well over a ton. "How long of a barrel are we talking?"

"I'm hoping ten feet."

"Hoping?"

"I don't have it yet. I wanted to make sure I got the right type of metal."

Part of Stoobs deflated. He'd become excited at the prospect of a big project filling the next day or so. But part of Stoobs was happy, too. At least the lady was worried about quality, not just some schwangled, donky fix that'd break the first time she used it. Plus, he could use the time in the interim to brush up on the fineries of cannon rifling.

"Mr. Stoobs, how much do you think this'll cost?"

"You can afford it."

"How much?"

"What ever you think is reasonable."

"I've never gotten a cannon barrel rifled."

"And I've never done one, so we're even on that."

"I have to pay you something."

"How about you cover my electricity, water, and telephone for the month? I own the building and I've got my food all figured out." Stoobs lightly kicked a plastic wrapped case of Vienna sausages under his workbench. "Sound fair?"

"Are you sure?" Shirley asked. "I didn't think you had a phone."

"Oh, I've got a phone. I just don't answer it." Shirley looked over to where Stoobs pointed, saw the phone, and noticed there was no answering machine.

Stoobs put on his glasses, sharpened a pencil with a knife that was handy, and wrote down the exact type of metal, where her best chances of getting it were, and the rough cost of it so she wouldn't be ripped off. He handed it to Shirley. "Here's what you need."

Shirley looked down at the note. It was written cleanly, efficiently, directly. That encouraged her. "Thanks, Mr. Stoobs."

"Don't thank me yet. I can still fuck it up. And it's just 'Stoobs.' I'm no 'mister.' So, why do you want to get all fancy and rifle the barrel? My figuring is that it's a pumpkin. Put enough force behind it and it'll go plenty quick in the direction you're shooting at."

"I actually want to hit what I'm aiming at. It's not purely for distance."

"Okey doke. Rifling'll help that, I suppose."

"I should be able to get the pipe within a couple of days. Will you be here around twelve-fifteen on Wednesday?" Shirley glanced at the walls and noticed there was no clock.

"Should be. If I'm not, just leave it by the door with your phone number. I tend to wander sometimes."

"See you soon," Shirley said.

"Yup." Stoobs unhinged the top of his sausages, and had forked another little pinkie of meat into his mouth by the time Shirley had made it back out into the parking lot.

CHAPTER TWENTY-SIX
Mortally Wounded by Work

Shirley had driven by the specialty metal supply warehouse thousands of times before, yet had never given it notice. It, too, was only a couple of miles away from her house. She realized the same happened whenever her routines were nudged a little—little things, like not noticing a neighbor's birdbath until spring when it became filled with playing and chirping White-throated Sparrows. After parking and making sure that she had tie-downs in the station wagon, Shirley walked into the warehouse. She scanned the tall aisles for ten minutes, then got the feeling that she was being ignored. The place was exceptionally quiet. She looked down at Stoobs' note and made her way to where most of the aluminum pipe was, stacked up in large racks. Tracing her fingers over their markings, she found the specific alloy she was looking for with the correct wall thickness. Taking a mental note of where she'd found what she was looking for, she walked back to the cash register. Behind it, a man sat, almost as limp as the noodle he was lazily slurping out of a cup of soup. "Hello," Shirley said timidly. "Hello, could you help me?"

The man huffed, slowly craned his neck back, looked at the clock, and said, "I've got two more minutes left on my break, lady."

"Is there anyone else here who can help me?"

"Nope. Curtis just left."

Shirley was in no mood to fight or push the issue—she was well trained, having served for so long in government jobs and with government co-workers—so she took a seat on the other side of the desk while the man finished his soup. They sat out of sight of one another for 120 seconds, then the man exhaled deeply as if work was about to mortally wound him, punched his time card without getting out of his seat, stood up, and said, "Yeah?"

"I'd like to buy some pipe," Shirley chimed.

"What're you looking for?"

"Here. It's all written down."

The man looked down at the note, squinted, looked at Shirley, then looked at the note again. "Yeah, we got it."

"I think it's in the third aisle," Shirley tried to help.

The man rounded the desk at the end of the register, still looking at the note. "Say, are you getting this for Stoobs?"

"Well, he's helping us make something," Shirley answered, surprised. "How'd you guess?"

"The handwriting. Stoobs knows his shit. What's he making?" The man's voice was flat, but he was making forward progress.

"Oh, he's just going to smooth out the inside of it," Shirley fibbed.

"What you gonna use it for? It's high grade stuff."

"I don't know," Shirley fibbed some more. "I'm getting it for my husband."

"Ten feet?"

"Yes."

"No returns on cut pipe."

"Fine," said Shirley.

The man walked past all the aisles, to the back of the warehouse, expertly removed a fifteen-foot length of pipe, plopped it on a dolly truck, rolled it over to the cutter, and measured it without talking to Shirley. He didn't put on safety goggles and sparks leapt all around his head as he made the cut in a single, fluid motion. He patted out a burning ember on his shirtsleeve, annoyed.

Shirley followed the man to the register. "Cash or charge?"

"Cash."

"Won't charge you for the cut. Plus, we had it surplus. Since you know Stoobs, you got a deal," the man said, his voice still had no inflection.

"Thanks," Shirley said as she carefully counted her money and placed it on the counter. Exact change. Just as she was going to ask the question, the man interrupted her. "Need me to get it into the parking lot?"

Shirley nodded. "That'd be nice. Thank you."

It didn't look like the man moved faster than a sloth, but in no time the pipe was snuggly fit into the station wagon. The end of it stuck out a couple of feet. "That should do it." He tapped it brusquely. It didn't move.

CHAPTER TWENTY-SEVEN
Two-Sentence Instructions

On Wednesday, at twelve-fifteen, Stoobs was pleased. The more modern life had advanced, the more people wanted to debate what wasn't debatable, like what goddamned time it was. They had problems following explicit directions, yet this lady in the goofy sweaters had brought exactly what he'd noted down. It even measured the right size.

"Fuckin' A," Stoobs said, slapping an adjacent wall. "You got it right." His voice was echoed since his lips were talking through an end of the pipe.

"I just handed over your note."

"Not that hard, was it?"

"Nope," Shirley answered.

"You'd be surprised how many people fuck up the simplest two-sentence instructions. You go to the place I suggested?" Stoobs took the pipe and effortlessly walked it through the doorway so it wouldn't bang against the frame.

"Yeah. A not-very-talkative guy helped me out."

"Kinda acts like he just got hit by a tranquilizer dart?"

"That'd be him."

"Randall. Works good, just don't like working." Stoobs had already set up his work area. "You interested in watching?"

Shirley looked at her watch. "I have a couple of minutes

before I have to get back to work."

"Shit, that'll give me time to load 'er up." Stoobs made a hand gesture for Shirley to follow him. The workshop was well lit. On the walls and benches were the internal body parts of scores of endangered mechanical species. The metal alloy manifolds, roller lifters, and harmonic balancers of DeSotos, Crockers, and Tuckers gleamed like vital organs on a surgeon's table, awaiting transplants.

Stoobs mounted the pipe into a gigantic vice and secured it. "See this?"

Shirley saw what looked like a wide, flattened spider with fingernail files for its feet.

"It's a modified cylinder borer. First off, we've got to make sure the inside's perfectly symmetrical. Gently buff out any burrs, dips, or peaks. Next, we'll do the actual rifling. The trick is to not cut so deep that'll shred your pumpkin when it exits—I mean, who the fuck wants mashed pumpkin? But the cuts have to be deep enough to give it some spin. Do all that right, and I should get you a hummer." Stoobs worked deliberately, with a machine-like efficiency. He was in no hurry, but rarely was he still. To Stoobs, every piece he made was the result of a carefully calculated series of predictable events. Bending over and eyeballing it one last time, he was sure everything was lined up properly.

"Stand back a couple of feet," Stoobs ordered as he donned a face guard and flicked a switch. High voltage electrical humming gave way to a gentle shower of sparks as the inside of the pipe was buffed smooth.

Before the machine had completely wound down, Stoobs flipped his mask up. "You know, what we're doing today was invented in Nuremberg around 1492. Cutting spiral grooves in a barrel. Nothing new. Very little is. The car you drove here today, its engine? The first four-stroke piston cycle internal combustion engine was built over one hundred years ago. May 1876, by a high school dropout named Nikolaus August Otto. He was a travelling salesman, I think."

Shirley shook her head slightly. She hadn't known any of that, but was fascinated.

Stoobs readjusted the spider, covered it with a cloth, and sent it down the barrel again. "Cleaning out any soot or errant shavings," he explained over the din.

"You know what a sine curve is?" Stoobs asked.

Shirley's ears were ringing a bit, so she yelled out her answer. "It's kind of like making a perfect circle, but over time—like the length of a pipe—so it's a helix."

Stoobs smiled. He was expecting "looptey loop" or something as scientific. Shirley was all right. "You got it. It provides the least amount of distortion. Encourages the spin, makes the projectile twist at the correct rate. Like, when quarterback throws a tight spiral. Those balls travel more true." As Stoobs was talking, he'd taken off the cloth, removed the grinding head, and, although he hadn't told Shirley this, he'd made a tool just for this job. Perfectly centered, it incorporated three equidistant, hardened, sharpened cutting wheels to make three simultaneous cuts in the barrel. It was a piece of sculpture that would earn its worth through work, not from being idle and perched on a pedestal in a museum. He affixed this to a lathe, which would push it down the barrel at a fixed rate of speed.

"We're gonna cut her at about 1/100ths of an inch each pass. No blasted idea how deep it should be for a pumpkin, figuring they're irregular and all, but I think I can wing it. What's important is that the groove's the same all the way down the barrel and the twist rate is uniform."

Shirley glanced down at her watch. "Stoobs." She successfully stifled calling him "Mister."

The old man didn't look up.

"Stoobs!"

His head raised.

"I'm sorry. I have to get back to work."

"You're going to miss the fun."

"I'm sorry."

"I should have 'er done by tomorrow."

"I can make it after work."

"Sure."

Right before her first step out of the shop, there was a horrible noise, like the single longest pull of a fingernail down a chalkboard, but to Shirley, it was beautiful. It was the future; the sound of pumpkins flying straight and true.

CHAPTER TWENTY-EIGHT
Ever Crash Land a B-17 Flying Fortress
in the Ocean?

"Ever crash land a B-17 Flying Fortress in the ocean?" Stoobs asked when Shirley entered his shop on Thursday, after a polite knock.

"Pardon?"

"Got to keep her level. Drop the ball turret. Keep the wheels up, ¾ flaps down. Make sure you open up all the doors and windows before you hit. Hold on tight. Approach the water at a real shallow angle so that you'll deflect upward, like a skipping rock. Luckily, it was a still day. Not even a ripple. We ended up just walking out on the wing with our rafts and radio and waited a couple of hours before being rescued. Hell, the water was even nice. No sharks. Barely got wet when we all could have easily died."

Shirley didn't know how to respond, so she fell back on her automatic response. She smiled.

"I think about that a lot," Stoobs said. "I thought about that when I was rifling your barrel. If you know what the worst is, and prepare for it, even if it comes, it may be on a day with nice, sunny weather, so it won't be so bad." Stoobs took the last sip of what looked like a once-full glass of whiskey. Clear tendrils of alcohol clung to the sides of the glass. "Any guesses as to what these are?"

Stoobs held up a thin, shiny piece of metal, much thinner

than dental floss. It hung in large spiral.

"A wire?" Shirley half guessed. She was tired from work, and although she liked Stoobs, she just really wanted to go home and decompress; maybe get some knitting in.

"Nope. That's the result of one continuous barrel rifling. It's like peeling the entire skin off an orange in one try. A ten-foot-long motherfucker of an orange."

"Wow." Shirley's surprise was genuine. There was no doubt the old man knew his stuff.

"I think she'll work nicely for you." Stoobs stood up, steadied himself with the edge of his desk, walked into his shop, and quickly returned with Shirley's barrel. "Didn't experience any problems."

Shirley looked inside the barrel. Ten feet of perfect-looking spirals. She fingered the artful grooves. "Wow," she repeated.

"Glad you like it," Stoobs said.

Shirley reached into her purse and placed some cash on the desk. It was merely a guess as to what Stoobs' utilities were.

"Cash money, I like. It don't bounce and you don't have to go to a bank to make it work." He handed Shirley back a twenty. "Thanks for doing what I asked you to do." He paused and waited for her to leave. "Shit, sorry. Would you like some help putting it in your car?"

"I've got it," Shirley said.

"Bull," Stoobs replied.

"That'd be great. I'd appreciate it."

Stoobs practically launched the pipe into the back of the station wagon, then Shirley secured it with the tie-downs.

"Can you do me a favor?" Stoobs asked as Shirley got behind the steering wheel.

"What is it?"

"Send me a picture when she's all done."

"Sure. It may be a bit. I've got a lot of work ahead of me," Shirley replied.

"Hell, I'm not goin' anywhere." Stoobs walked back inside, opened up the top drawer of his desk, unscrewed the cap from the bottle, and poured himself another tall glass. He finished a sentence well after Shirley had left. "Everyone promises pictures."

Quietly, Stoobs' mind tilted to a long-ago horizon, where he was busy hammering away at the rust-frozen safety nuts that needed to be removed for the turret ball to drop. He had to hurry—they were running low on fuel—swearing that if he just had a socket wrench, the right tool at the right time, they probably weren't all going to die in the waters of the South Pacific.

He felt safest amongst his machines.

CHAPTER TWENTY-NINE
Three White Diamonds

If there was ever a governing body—say, like that which oversees kung fu and earning a black belt—Shirley would have been the regional champion for garage saling. Her skill was as much patience and diligence as knowing when to strike. She knew how low a price could be leg-swept without being insulting. Weather permitting, Shirley began riding her bike to every sale. She would return in the station wagon if she purchased something too large to lug home on the bike. She almost always wore bulky clothes. But just like the musculature of a sheepdog underneath a thick mat of fur, Shirley developed strong muscles under her loose-fitting pants and sweaters.

As Shirley rifled through countless chipped plates, toys with missing appendages, dusty exercise equipment with low miles clocked on their odometers, water-damaged books, pet-chewed furniture, anonymous stains in improbable places, and things she couldn't imagine anyone ever buying—like a torn-off bumper of a car with its license plate still attached—she quietly accumulated her arsenal.

Garage sales are the soft cousin to despair and excess. Either someone was getting rid of something because they were upgrading, were out of room, or, on occasion, a loved one had just died, and their worldly possessions were being liquidated and the surviving members of the family doing the selling didn't really know what they had on their hands. Shirley liked those sales the most. That's where the gold was. Older people tended to hold onto materials and tools that were designed to last more than just a couple of years.

Gold for Shirley came in the form of entire welding rigs, an industrial air compressor, angle iron, the chassis for ten-foot long trailer, most of a tandem bicycle, huge air reservoir tanks, lengths of chain, a big disk of wood, tempered steel drill bits, and pressure gauges. Shirley thought that with the right set of eyes and finely honed barter reflexes, almost anyone could build a pumpkin cannon for pennies on the dollar. Coming home from a particularly fruitful run, before Shirley's keys finished sliding across the kitchen counter, she saw three stark, white pumpkins lined up in tandem to her bright yellow measuring ball.

Rachel, giddy, bounded into the kitchen on stocking feet and pulled a pirouette on the linoleum. "Ta-da!"

"So, these are the pumpkins you've been growing?"

"Yup!"

"They're strong?"

"Strongest yet." Rachel made he-man muscle builder motions with her arms and flexed playfully.

"May I?" Shirley motioned to pick one up.

"Be my guest."

Shirley picked up the pumpkin and thwacked it really hard. "It's not very hollow."

"Tiny seed cavity. Heavy on the meat and rind. The meat's like muscle: fibrous and can take quite a shock."

"The rind is sort of waxy. It's also very smooth." The pumpkins looked more like bowling balls with cropped stems than any sort of pumpkin Shirley had seen at any roadside fruit and vegetable stand.

"I figured it wouldn't hurt to have some sort of natural

lubrication. Ease of loading plus in-flight stability," Rachel offered.

"How do you know that it's not brittle, just dense?"

"Drop it," Rachel coaxed.

"No. Not in the kitchen."

"I'll clean it up." Rachel clapped her hands together in excitement. "If it breaks. I'll pick up all the mess. Promise."

"No. Really? Surely, it'll break."

"Drop it from waist high."

Palms already sweating, Shirley dropped the pumpkin. Instead of the crunchy, hollow cave-in sound she was expecting, it just sort of dropped and hit with very little noise at all, like it had fallen onto foam padding. Shirley picked the pumpkin up. There were no cracks, just a slight flat spot where the pumpkin had hit the ground.

Rachel smiled an incredibly wide smile. "I'm calling them 'White Diamonds.' Hardest pumpkin around. You're not the only one who's got a trick or two up her sleeve."

"You didn't inject it with anything when it was growing? Resin? Plastic? Anything?"

"C'mon, grandma. That'd be cheating," Rachel said. "One hundred percent natural genetics. No foreign substances. Just gene splicing, tons of experiments, and greenhousing. That's it. When the time comes, I can probably make about thirty a pop."

"How'd you get them to grow so uniform?"

"After they get big enough, I have a round cage I put them into. They still get nutrients and sunlight, but they can only grow to that size. That's why the rind is so smooth. It fills itself out."

"Remarkable. Simply remarkable," Shirley glowed. She still wasn't expecting such perfect organic ammunition as she pulled out a cloth measuring tape from a drawer and the pumpkin's circumference was exactly that of the rubber ball's. Her fingers excitedly thrummed the pumpkin. "Rachel, thank you. I'm so proud of you." The two hugged. "Say, hey, can you help me out with a bike

I got today? It's in the back of the station wagon."

Even though the bicycle's front wheel was so badly bent that it couldn't rotate and the frame was slight rusty, Rachel didn't ask what the tandem bicycle was for. She wanted to be surprised, just like what she'd just done to her grandma.

CHAPTER THIRTY
An Arrow from Outer Space

The decision to make a human-powered cannon came from the sky and implanted itself directly in the middle of Shirley's brain, like an arrow from outer space.

Shirley had picked up knitting at an early age—four or five, she couldn't quite remember—and her fingers had become fleet. Her eyes were accustomed to intricate detail. She would know if a stitch wasn't right just by a quick feel. She knew how much yarn she had left without even looking. She knew by the slack of it coming loose from the spool.

And so, when Shirley took to teaching herself welding, in her hands, the two activities weren't as different as one might expect. Sure, there was incredible heat involved—flames that could cut through an eighth inch of steel as easily as a finger through whipped topping—but Shirley's senses quickly adjusted to the new medium. Her practice welds were clumpy, splotchy, irregular. But in no time, learning the nuance of the flame and that different thicknesses and types of metal heated differently, her welds became strong and beautiful: good penetration; ample fusion and proper fill; minimal distortion; and no splatter. They looked as silky as cream cheese smoothed on a bagel and held like the dickens.

She wanted the cannon to be mobile and secure, so the first

153

order of business had been converting a motorcycle trailer into the carriage. It was essentially a flat ten-foot long, eight-foot wide rectangle on wheels. It was perfect. To that, she welded two heavy angle iron triangles, which stood two feet tall, over each of the wheel wells. It looked like the skeleton of a seesaw when she mounted a large plate between the two triangles. On the tops of the triangles were eyelets. A rod welded to the bottom of the sheet of metal was run through both of the eyelets. The idea was that she could tilt the barrel's elevation. To the rear of the plate, she welded on pegs and fastened four heavy-duty truck shock absorbers, then attached the elevated metal plate to the carriage. Although not lickety-split quick, with several turns of a wrench, the shock absorbers could be expanded and contracted so the large metal plate could tilt backwards or forwards. It didn't need to move more than several degrees. Shirley also hoped that they would help absorb some of the recoil.

There are moments during invention that are delicate and perishable. There are other moments during invention that seem to be made of steel, and it's sometimes impossible to know where these ideas came from.

Halfway through welding a mount so the bike could be quickly attached and removed from the carriage, she took her hand off of the trigger of the torch, flipped up her welding mask, and began talking to herself, an activity she found herself doing more and more. "What could be the worst anyone could say? 'Look at that dumpy broad huffing and puffing on her tiny pumpkin pumper.'" That's it? That's all they can say?" Shirley had dialogues and dramas with herself. Partly in preparation. Partly because if she really did become her harshest critic, she had nothing else to worry about.

Shirley looked down at her grease pencil measurements for the mount. Everything still appeared straight. Flipping the mask back down, reaching for the flint igniter, and bringing the flame to a sharp, bright blue tongue, she finished the job. Joining metallic parts through the application of heat had become little different to Shirley than joining loops of a continuous yarn into a Kitchener stitch. When objects ended up in her hands, they became more intimate. United.

CHAPTER THIRTY-ONE
The Sound of a Gigantic Airplane
Toilet Flushing

"How do you feel about bike riding?" Shirley asked.

"I'm okay with it." Rachel looked up from her book.

"Want to follow me?"

"Sure."

Shirley led her granddaughter to the garage and let her get a good look.

"I don't get it," Rachel said as she glanced over what her grandma had constructed.

At first, Shirley thought she'd finish the entire cannon and unveil it only moments before hitching it to the back of the station wagon and firing off a couple rounds, but she came to the conclusion that she needed a second pair of legs.

"It's not even a cannon yet," Rachel continued, then stopped, when she saw the fragile and slightly pained expression on her grandma's face.

Shirley grimaced while trying to smile. She was aware that three months had passed since the beginning of construction and there wasn't a huge amount of progress to the naked eye. Her granddaughter couldn't see the invisible pillars of pneumatics and kinetic energy holding the cannon-in-progress together.

"Let me take you through it. It's a little closer to being done.

The barrel won't be mounted until the very end."

"Why's that?" Rachel asked quickly.

"I don't think I'll be able to close the garage door. It'll be a tight fit if it does." Shirley cleared her throat. "Here's what will have to happen for the pumpkin to leave the barrel at an acceptable velocity. Take a seat."

Shirley put on her gold-flecked football helmet and she gave Rachel a green one. "Put this on." Shirley had cut pieces of clear plastic, which served as eye shields, and zip-tied them to the helmets. "Just on the outside chance everything blows up."

"Really?"

"Slim chance."

Rachel looked at her grandma to see if she was joking. She came to the conclusion that Shirley was concentrating. Rachel sat down on the front seat of the tandem bike. Instead of having a front wheel, the front hub was attached to the carriage by a neat and simple homemade lock. "Nice padding." She wiggled her butt in the seat.

"Oh, I just stuffed some more foam in it. The other seat was a little too hard and athletic. I like a little cushioning," Shirley said with obvious pride in her workmanship. She had also learned the trick that, when hitting some roadblocks in development, it's always a good idea to have some smaller, conquerable side projects on the back burner.

"Okay, so what's this?" Rachel asked, tapping the thirty-six inch diameter particleboard disk that was bolted directly below her onto the bicycle's steel chainwheel.

"Put your feet on the pedals, into the toe clips," Shirley instructed.

Rachel did as she was told.

"Start pedaling."

The pedals were attached to the three-foot wide disc, which spun true. Shirley had routed a groove on the edge of the particleboard, which had then been lined with thin rubber straps to prevent slippage. The rubber straps also prevented the chain from wearing through the wood. Rachel began pedaling with ease. The other end of the chain connected the large disc to an exposed gear on an air compressor. A set of pedals, for the second rider on the tandem bike, spun ghostily behind her.

"Take it easy," Shirley said. "You're not in a race."

Rachel slowed down to a comfortable pace.

"Here's what's happening. The disk is acting like a flywheel. We're taking advantage of its weight, converting bike pedaling into air pressure. Your legs are creating torque, which is just a measurement of how much force it takes to cause an object to rotate."

"It's rotating," Rachel replied.

"It is. But when I just attached the little sprocket that was originally on the bicycle directly to the air compressor. Human legs make jerky torque. When you pedal, see how you sway a little left and right? We're not as predictable as machines, which, among other things, can result in a lot of stress on the parts. So, by attaching the original sprocket to a big flywheel, the torque is smoothed out considerably. It absorbs part of the energy when you're cranking down on the pedals and releases it in that tiny bit of dead time your legs are getting in position again."

"Grandma, how did you think this up?"

"My mother had a pedal-powered sewing machine when I was growing up. It kind of went from there." Shirley pointed to a gauge. A red needle was slowly, steadily rising on the white face of its dial, eking past small, black numbers. "See that?"

Rachel followed her grandmother's finger, away from the rotating flywheel, along the chain, to a nearby sprocket, then nodded.

"That's an air compressor. What you're doing now is using this," Shirley tapped the compressor, "to fill up these." Shirley tapped two canisters. "Air reservoirs. Think of it as pumping up an extremely large bicycle tire that can hold 400 gallons of air, until it explodes all at once," Shirley gave one of the air canisters a heavy nudge to make sure it wasn't loose, "except we predict, control, and direct the explosion."

Rachel kept pedaling.

Shirley looked at the gauge while slowly running her hands over the thick, metal-braided hoses, which connected the compressor to the reservoirs, checking for leaks at the connection points. All of the nipples, fittings, and Teflon tape had done their jobs. "Fifty p.s.i. Not bad." She looked at her stopwatch. It had been a little over seventy seconds.

"Did you know that in metric, torque isn't measured in foot-pounds, but in 'Newton-meters'?"

"How could I have known that?" Rachel had barely broken a sweat and her breathing was normal.

"And that Newton was the first scientist ever to be knighted for his work?" The stopwatch ticked to ninety seconds. "Hit the actuator valve now," Shirley ordered.

Rachel looked at her grandmother. "The whaty what?"

"Push that big, red button," Shirley instructed. "And keep it down for a couple of seconds."

An exhaled sneeze of air violently rattled the windowpanes in the garage door fifteen feet away, and blew a corridor of dust off the floor. The carriage rocked slightly in its stabilizers.

"Good." Shirley nodded and made several notations in her notebook. "That button is attached to a butterfly valve. It does a good job of releasing, all at once, the pressure that you've built up." Shirley's fingers brushed the surface of where all the air had just been discharged. She rubbed her fingers with her thumb. Just what she was hoping for: the slightest bit of lubricating oil. "You can stop pedaling now." Rachel twisted her feet out of the pedals, which rotated several times on their own before stopping.

"That kind of sounded like a gigantic airplane toilet flushing."

Shirley smiled again. "It does have more of a sucking sound than I expected." To Shirley, it was a perfect and beautiful sound.

As Rachel stood up, the two clonked their helmets together awkwardly, in triumph. It seemed like the right thing to do.

"Be courageous and steady to the laws and you cannot fail!" Shirley exalted.

"Are you quoting Isaac Newton?"

"Guilty as charged." Shirley's cheeks flushed under the protection of her helmet. "Thanks for helping."

"That's it?" Rachel asked. "I can pedal some more."

"Not now. Thanks."

CHAPTER THIRTY-TWO
The Velocity of Junk

The next several weeks, brimming with a recharged enthusiasm that everything was going to plan, Shirley positioned the five-foot-long water main that the barrel would be welded to, double checked her measurements, and then welded the two large parts together until they were one. The heavy surplus sewer line was slightly thinner than the barrel, less than an eighth of an inch, so that when a pumpkin was loaded, it would stop at the correct place.

Using a winch and pulley system, Shirley was able to lift the barrel up and then weld it directly to the elevated metal plate on the carriage.

The water main already had an inlet valve on its side and it was a cinch to install the butterfly valve to it.

It finally looked like a cannon. It fit in the garage by barely an inch.

Shirley busied herself with making more restraints along the length of the barrel so it wouldn't flex too much or buck back when it was fired.

She spot-welded some old rifle sights that she'd found in a junk drawer at a yard sale onto the barrel. The rear sight was little more than a slide rule the military had adopted for aiming high-powered rifles.

Shirley itched to fire it. She knew she was in a residential neighborhood, but she also guessed that whatever she shot would go directly down the street and the street didn't end for over a quarter of a mile. All she'd have to do is ride her bike to where the projectile stopped and do the calculations using the bike's odometer. Easy as pie.

She rolled up the garage door and anxiously searched for something harmless to launch. Nothing hard. Nothing dangerous. Just a quiet little test fire at three on a Sunday afternoon.

"Who'd notice? What'd be the harm?" Shirley asked herself, acutely aware she was about to use a homemade cannon to fire a projectile down a residential street.

Rifling through drawer after drawer, realizing that a lot of the non-essential things in her house were an awful lot like the discards she passed over in garage sales countless times, she found a rubber chicken.

"When did I buy a rubber chicken?" Shirley idly asked herself. Then, "A rubber chicken! That'll work."

She used a pole vault pole—again from a garage sale—with a mop head screwed to the end of it, to ram some plastic grocery bags down the barrel. They created a nice seal. Next came the chicken. After taking another glance down the road to double check no one was coming, Shirley donned her football helmet and began pedaling. All of the gauges, switches, and dials were handily in front of her, just like an instrument panel in a car. She pedaled for ten minutes and watched the p.s.i. climb, climb, climb up to 200. Her palms were sweaty underneath her leather gloves. Blood thrummed behind her ears. She went to push her glasses back onto the bridge of her nose, but instead hit the plastic face shield on the helmet. She felt electric.

"This is it!" she yelled to herself. She shot her arm out and pressed the big red button. The cannon bucked with a whoosh. The blocks in front of and in back of the tires did their job. A large plume of white vapor rushed out of the barrel. The p.s.i.

returned to zero. Shirley twisted her feet out of the pedals and hopped on her bike, resetting the odometer. She kept her eyes focused on the ground as she pedaled. Adrenaline surged through her, intoxicating her like she'd just drank a whole bottle of root beer schnapps in one gulp. As she neared where the road "T"d off and ended, she still hadn't located the chicken.

"Mother crusher! Melon baller!" Shirley yelled, crestfallen. "This is bulljive!"

Horrible thoughts screeched across Shirley's mind. What if the chicken hadn't even left the cannon? What if it was still in the barrel? She hadn't seen it leave. All she'd seen was white vapor and now there was no chicken on the road. Surprised to hear a truck approaching, Shirley composed herself. It was quite all right if she considered herself crazy and quite another thing entire if other people came to the same conclusion. She quickly removed the football helmet she'd forgotten to take off.

Thompson, her neighbor, slowed his pickup truck as he neared, and rolled down his window. "Hey Shirl, nice day for a bike ride," he said politely.

"Sure is."

Thompson nodded. That was all he had planned in the way of conversation. His gaze shifted from Shirley on the bike, to about two feet over her head, ten feet back. He pushed his base-ball hat back on his head. His face screwed up and he put his truck in park. Shirley spun and followed Thompson while his cowboy boots crunched gravel as he walked towards a tree.

The rubber chicken was almost totally imbedded in the bark of a giant white oak. Thompson flicked open a penknife, plucked at the chicken's rubbery beak, then scratched his chin. It was most definitely a rubber chicken. "Don't see that every day, now do you?" Thompson asked.

Shirley tried to remain nonchalant, but inside she was doing back flips on a high wire. "No, you sure don't."

Thompson got in his truck, tipped his hat to Shirley, then

drove off.

"1,324 feet." Shirley mentally slapped herself on the back. "Not bad, old girl."

Shirley walked back to her house, ebullient, not quite believing her success. Her theory had catapulted over being a proof and had instantly been confirmed as a scientific law. Shirley swirled in a dance, pretending her workshop was a ballroom and Newton's laws were really Newton's own body. Distance, displacement, speed, velocity, acceleration, force, mass, momentum, energy, work, and power swirled all around her mind in joyful strands of lights.

After the dance, Shirley thoroughly inspected the cannon, expecting it to have had degenerated in some shape or form. She shined a flashlight down the barrel to see if any foreign material was stuck in it, inspected the welds for fatigue, and checked the carriage's tire pressure. "Tip top," Shirley said, then pulled the garage door down.

She played nonchalant when Rachel got home from studying.

"What's up, grandma?"

"Nothing," Shirley answered, but her smile gave her away immediately.

"What? Is it done?"

"Better."

"It works?"

Smile.

"How do you know?"

Smile.

"You tested it?"

Smile.

"Where?"

Smile.

"From the garage?"

Smile.

"No, from the garage? What'd you shoot?" Rachel was happy to see this reckless side to her grandma.

Shirley's smile couldn't have been pecked off her face by vultures. "I know this sounds cryptic, but I want you to be surprised. Ride down the road and when it dead ends, look in the trees, about head height."

"Okay?"

Moments later: "A motherfuckin' chicken?" Rachel asked the tree, knowing she was well out of her grandmother's earshot. She gripped the rubbery body and released it in a quick snap when it wouldn't let go of the trunk. The chicken was thoroughly fused into the wood. "No fuckin' way. Go grandma!"

Several hours after that first successful launch, the plastic grocery bags which had been used as wadding continued floating on air currents, gliding like slow-moving, white birds, high above Shirley's neighborhood. They wouldn't land for quite some time.

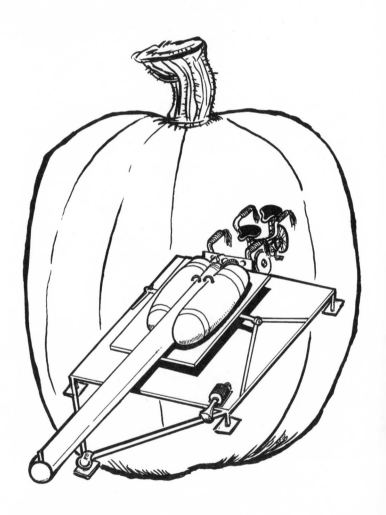

CHAPTER THIRTY-THREE
The Honking Trunk of a Pink Elephant

Details, details, details. Although the cannon had fired without any noticeable flaw or problem and had tested beyond expectation, there was more to consider. One couldn't just drive down the road towing a cannon and not arouse suspicion or break some uptight law made to protect decent society.

After careful measuring, Shirley first cut, then sewed large swatches of heavy canvas. The cover should hide bulk, but not flap too violently in the wind at cruising speeds when being towed. After fitting it and covering the cannon, Rachel said exactly what her grandma was thinking. "It kinda looks like we're smuggling Snuffleupagus."

Early in the morning, the station wagon's automatic transmission, although strong, heaved through the gears, burdened not only by the usual weight of Shirley and Rachel, but by the weight of the cannon and twenty pumpkins. They saw very few cars. Mist hung heavy, making the sun appear dull.

The startling white pumpkins jiggled in milk crates, resembling bleached and featureless doll heads more than any type of vegetable.

Rachel helped her grandmother remove the tarp, folded it into a neat square, and tucked it into the station wagon. Then she took a step back, waiting for Shirley to motion her for an extra hand, which she lent when the bicycle was bolted into position.

Shirley checked dials, tapped tanks, tested the tension of chains.

"Mind carrying the pole, a level, and a ruler?"

Rachel shook her head, used the pole as a walking stick, and stuck the level and ruler in opposite back pockets of her tight-fitting jeans.

"Mind counting along with me?"

Rachel shook her head again.

Using a bicycle wheel—that had a fluorescent orange dot spray-painted on the rim at one point on the tire—attached to a pole, Shirley quietly counted the number of rotations as she walked away from the muzzle of the cannon. Rachel walked parallel with her, quietly counting in her head. They walked quite a distance until they came to a dirt berm over twenty feet high.

"How many did you count?"

Rachel's number matched Shirley's and she wrote it neatly down on her notebook.

"Pole, please."

Shirley jammed the pole into the ground, down to the first spray-painted mark near its tip. It stood up straight. Shirley made another notation.

"Level, please."

She balanced the small level on top of the pole. With a few minor tugs and bumps, the bubble in the level's green fluid steadied between two marks. She then removed the level, unpocketed the laser that had been used in the potato cannon, and rested it on top of the pole so it shone a dot on the berm.

"Honey, would you spray paint a little dot exactly where the laser's hitting?" Shirley asked, handing Rachel a can of fluorescent orange paint while snapping off the cap with her thumb.

Rachel did as she was asked.

"How good are you with drawing circles?"

"Pretty good." Rachel took out the ruler, laid one end on the dot she'd already sprayed, and sprayed four more dots at the other end, turning the ruler ninety degrees after each one. She then connected the dots, making a darn near perfect four-foot-wide circle.

"That's good. Can you fill it all in?"

Rachel did.

Shirley turned off the laser and removed the pole from the ground. She then pulled a pocket altimeter out of her satchel and wrote down the elevation. Although the ground wasn't perfectly even, the cannon's barrel was essentially level with the middle of the circle Rachel had sprayed.

"Count back with me, just to be sure?"

The distance was the same so Shirley didn't make a notation.

"Want to know what I'm doing?" Shirley asked as she thrust the pole into the ground, right in front of the cannon's barrel.

"Sure."

"There are other forces at work." She looked at the tops of trees for wind, which were still. "But the main one is gravity. The further away we launch a pumpkin, the more we're going to have to angle the barrel upward. What I'm doing is making sure the barrel's at the same height as that target." She looked at the spray painted mark near the top of the pole, just to be triple sure. "It is." She then climbed up on the cannon, making sure her weight was directly over the carriage's axles. "Then I need to make sure that the cannon's level."

Shirley placed the level on the barrel. She made some minor adjustments, wrenching the shock absorbers in the back ever so slightly.

"Oh, pooh," Shirley said. "I forgot we had to aim it first." She looked through the sights, one eye closed, the other squinting. "No kidding." As far as she could tell, the cannon was pointing directly at the middle of the gauzy orange circle in the distance. "Looks like we're good to go." Shirley pulled out two pink, hard plastic seats from the rear of the station wagon. Rachel retrieved the pole vault pole and went back for a crate of pumpkins.

The pumpkins fit perfectly, just like they had in the dry tests at home. Just a little bit of friction for a great seal. "These are such a perfect size, honey."

Rachel smiled.

"So, as it's set up right now, I know it's going to miss. Since the barrel is at exactly the same height, and I'm shooting in a straight line, how far ahead of the target the pumpkin hits will tell me how much gravity is affecting it."

"Sounds good to me," Rachel said as she took it all in, understanding about half of what her grandmother was talking about, but trusting what she said.

They stretched their muscles for five minutes. Rachel had been warned there'd be a lot of exercise.

They both put on their helmets, then got on the tandem bike and started pedaling. The flywheel spun, the air compressor turned, the air reservoirs filled with greater and greater air pressure.

"Just ten more seconds," Shirley yelled, not knowing how easy it was for Rachel to hear her. The pressure hit 200 p.s.i. Shirley rang the bell affixed to the handlebars, which was the signal to slip their feet from the pedals. The flywheel spun without them as Shirley reached out and pressed the button. The cannon fired, sending a shock wave through the seats and a vapor trail of white through the air. Rachel felt an enticing vibration of power pulse through her arms and thighs as the pumpkin launched. Neither one of them could be sure that they saw the pumpkin actually leave the barrel and both of them desperately wanted to say that they did.

"That was frickin' cool, grandma!"

"Isn't it?" Shirley smiled, keeping her eyes on all of the gauges, making sure that her beast had exhaled properly.

Shirley wrote some figures down on her notebook. With the two of them, they only had to pedal for three minutes. Neither one of them was winded. They were pedaling at a doable fifteen miles per hour.

Shirley scouted the pumpkin with a pair of binoculars. It had fallen in front of the target. "Want to go for another walk?"

Again, they both counted the times the homemade measuring wheel rotated until they got to the pumpkin carcass. It was smeared and mangled at the end of a short rut in the soft ground. Having never seen a human head broken wide open, Rachel thought that's what the pumpkin looked like: white skull, orange brains. It was broken, but it wasn't completely scrambled.

"Considering the amount of force we're putting behind it, that was a wonderful launch," Shirley said as she closely examined the newly exposed orange meat of the pumpkin. "You've done a great job. Made mine easier, that's for sure."

Shirley didn't double-check her distance on the way back, plugged her numbers into a parabolic equation, showed Rachel how to adjust the shock absorbers, and stopped her when the level on top of the barrel showed an incline of four degrees.

Pumpkin after pumpkin after pumpkin jolted from the barrel of the cannon. They got closer with each successive volley and the women began to take longer breaks to recover from the pedaling. Their eyes were adjusting and could now catch the smallest glimpses of the airborne pumpkins.

After the tenth shot, Shirley saw that they had a bull's-eye on their hands. A tuft of upturned brown soil dotted the middle of the orange target. "We got it," she said in triumph, handing the binoculars over to Rachel for verification.

"Can't get better than that!" Rachel let out a little squeal.

They shot the eleventh pumpkin but couldn't find it. Jubilation turned into doubt.

They shot the twelfth pumpkin and it was the same result. Doubt turned into fear.

What if, Shirley thought, we're launching them over the berm? What if, Shirley thought further, I really don't know what I'm doing, that I'm just kidding myself?

171

"Do you see anything, honey?" Shirley tried to keep her voice flat as she handed the binoculars over to Rachel.

Rachel took a few seconds, straining her eyes. "No. Sorry, I don't." She really wanted to lie.

"Want to go for a look with me?"

They didn't measure. Shirley scanned nearby trees. The tingling from the cannon seemed to have gotten into Rachel's femurs and it felt good. She couldn't fully concentrate, looking for pumpkins. She didn't have the eye that her grandma did, who knew the exact location of the ones they'd previously launched and had scuttled into the earth. They walked all the way to the berm. Shirley cursorily glanced at the remnants of the one that had hit the bull's-eye and continued trudging up the embankment, hoping that her pumpkins didn't go off and kill someone.

Rachel stopped to look at their bull's-eye handiwork. Just as her grandma could sight a half-assed stitch in a quilt from across the room, Rachel intimately knew what was inside her pumpkins. She bent over and tenderly pushed some rind out of the way. Strings of pumpkin meat held on to seeds as she lifted a nearly complete rind. Using both hands, she took out parts of a pumpkin and put them aside. With a little more reconstruction, she puzzled together a second pumpkin, exposing a third one, virtually intact, impacted a good foot and a half in the giving earth.

"Grandma!" Rachel shouted.

Shirley dropped her gaze from the valley below, busily imagining a child knocked completely off of his bicycle, blood streaming from his head. She turned towards her granddaughter.

"They're all right here. They all hit the same place."

It would be hard to conceive of pumpkins flying more true, but there they were. Three different pumpkins had hit the bull's eye. No magic tricks. Shirley was shocked at first, filled with disbelief.

"No, honey. It's okay if we don't find them."

"Grandma, look."

Shirley's brain registered what her eyes were seeing: three different pumpkins, smashed, all lined up. Then she began to cry out of joy. Rachel started crying too because her grandma was so happy.

They leaned on each other as they walked back to the cannon.

"Remind me to send a picture to Stoobs," Shirley said as they got back to the station wagon.

Shirley was drained as they methodically disassembled the parts of the cannon for transit and re-covered it with the tarp for the drive home.

When Shirley got behind the wheel, her eyes puffy from victory, she honked the horn for a long, long time in celebration before putting the car into drive and slowly letting off the brake.

The two returned to the test range several times. They were never able to replicate the triple bull's-eye, but they were both becoming more confident and proficient in their artillery expertise. They could pedal faster and for longer periods of time. Shirley's aim was always within five feet of the target and she became a pro at gauging the wind.

At the end of a twenty-pumpkin session, Shirley popped a question to Rachel that she'd been wanting to ask for a long time. "Rache, do you think you could paint everything pink, except the barrel?" The "gunliness" of the cannon had become too much for her. What she'd made wasn't a weapon of destruction. It wasn't designed to inflict grievous harm. It was a release. It was the ethereal made into steel. It was a dream, made not of a mysterious blend of rainbows, unicorns, and gumdrops, but of welds, garage sale finds, and tight pneumatic seals. A thing of joy and physics. A ticket to enter a big dance.

"That'd be rad," Rachel responded. "But only if you do me a favor."

"Name it."

"Can you knit me a sweater with a skull in it for the competition?"

Shirley hesitated.

"It can be bright—like a pink sweater with an orange skull."

Shirley wasn't enthused, but agreed. "Sure. That sounds like a deal."

The paintjob took a full day, even after masking all of the sensitive parts. It dried overnight. When they removed the tape and newspaper, it looked like a modern sculpture—a pink elephant with its trunk honking straight out—and it made them both laugh.

Shirley looked up from a just-knitted sweater arm, put it down, and peered into the garage.

"It's so pink and girlie!"

CHAPTER THIRTY-FOUR
New Holes in a Rusted Duster

When Shirley had filled out the application form and sent it in months prior, the episode didn't feel quite real. Nor did the acceptance letter to the third annual pumpkin chuck. The drive to Delaware had been cautious but uneventful. Shirley felt more like she was watching a movie of herself do things than actually moving around. The reality of the situation of being on a field amongst her competitors—knowing fully well that she would not only be in the open, but watched and scrutinized—made her feel raw. It was almost too much stimuli. She coped, auto-piloted, by following her meticulous plan, step by step, which created this clear, tough shell that protected her.

Sampson, of Sampson and Sons Towing, the head official of that day's events, drove by on an ATV. "We'll just be firing down the line. You've got five minutes to load and fire your cannon after me and my men give you the sign."

Shirley nodded. Her hands were sweating. They were in the middle of the line of launchers. It'd be another forty-five minutes, at least, before they'd shoot.

In a sudden wave, Shirley's eyes sparked. Her gaze focused with flinty concentration. Like a hammer through a glass table, the shell around her shattered. Hibernation had ended. It would soon be time to get in the front seat and pedal the experiment as far as it could go.

"Want to go watch other folks launch? See how they do it?" Rachel asked.

"One or two wouldn't hurt."

All of the launching devices—catapults, trebuchets, and onagers—were made mostly out of hardwoods, with a metal spring here, a metal winch there, and garage door springs straining to capacity over there. No sign of another pneumatic cannon. Once launching started, it was like watching a slow, soft siege of a 16th-Century field. Pumpkins loped into the air and smashed into the ground. Some of them went reasonably far, flirting with the range of an outhouse on a pickup six hundred yards away.

With each successive launch she watched, Shirley became more confident.

Right before she turned to Rachel to say they should start with their pre-flight preparations, she watched a pumpkin tumble skyward into a flock of ducks, knocking one of them in mid-flight. It plummeted to the ground and flopped flat upon impact, obviously dead. The pumpkin launcher, a man in a viking helmet and bits of animal pelts hanging off of his thick belt, let out a groan of disbelief at his bad luck. The horns of his helmet dipped forward in shame as the game warden, under obligation to arrest him on the spot for hunting out of season, made the pantomime motions that he didn't want to do it, but the viking had to get in the back of the warden's 4x4.

An official-looking, pert, and clean woman entered the throng. Whispers quickly reached Shirley and Rachel at the edge of the group. "It's the Governess of Delaware," they said into their hands. "She hasn't missed a pumpkin chuck yet." The woman took the fish and game officer aside. The viking was released from the back of the Bronco shortly after. He had been issued a pardon. Cheers rumbled through the crowd. Beers cracked open. It was barely ten AM.

Shirley triple-tested the valves, gauges, dials, and chain tensions. She measured the barrel's angle. She kept an eye on the wind. They stretched for an extra five minutes. She visualized the launch over and over again.

"Grandma! They're giving us the signal."

Sampson and his men were in a pickup, far off to the side of the field. One of them flapped a bright orange flag.

"Ready?"

Rachel answered by putting on her helmet and clapping her grandma's shoulder. They loaded the pumpkin and began pedaling.

The next three minutes of pedaling was a soft white light of focus. Shirley could see the both of them, churning away. It was if she was floating high above the field. What separated their cannon from that far-off, broken-down car was a straight line: a fundamental element of physics.

Shirley and Rachel became semi-gloss sweaty. Their hearts raced. They continued pedaling with a trained intensity.

The pressure gauge hit 200 p.s.i., and in a treat to Rachel, Shirley hit a new, secret switch. A boat horn roared its airy warning that things were about to get interesting, the crowd turned en masse, then Shirley hit the button that activated the cannon.

A fifteen-pound pumpkin, as white as a full moon on a cloudless night, blasted through the trunk panels of a 1970 Dodge Duster that had been abandoned in a field years prior. Speeding along at an estimated nine hundred miles per hour, that white-rinded pumpkin screamed in such a shallow arc—almost a straight line, really—to the rusted Duster that it didn't look real. It looked more like a fat, white laser, not a pulpy gourd, as it whizzed over previously launched pumpkins, towards its own pumpkin mortality.

Shirley jumped up and down and whispered "Yay!" so very quietly that only Rachel heard her. Shirley clenched her fists and bowed her head in humility and thankfulness. She'd accomplished what she'd set out to do.

Shirley removed her helmet. Muted tines of steam rose from her head as she looked at the hole in the car through a pair of binoculars. Sunlight gleamed through the hole that she'd just made. She could see clear through the trunk. To verify she wasn't just seeing what she wanted to see, she motioned her granddaughter to take a look. The binoculars were already pre-focused on the Duster, 2,640 feet away. Half a mile. It was a distance that few pumpkin chuckers in the world could reach—let alone participants in a rural Delaware competition—but no one had ever launched a pumpkin right on through a car from that far away. It was almost inconceivable. Impossible. The car had been there for the two previous years of the contest, just sitting there rusting, acting as a trellis for weeds.

Shirley began to notice a buzzy murmur from the audience and fellow competitors. Many stopped sipping their complimentary apple cider for a second, not quite sure how to process what they may or may not have seen.

Although not quite as serious as Galileo's plight to convince the Roman Catholic Church that the earth wasn't the center of the universe, Shirley had just ripped off the fuzzy seat of the pumpkin launching world's pants and placed on the top of its head like a raccoon skin cap. Many of Shirley's competitors felt the stirrings of an emotional cocktail that began with incredulity, envy, and inadequacy and ended in confusion. Catapults felt medieval. Trebuchets' pivoted beams seemed to sag. Their siege for supremacy had ended. There was a new way to throw a pumpkin.

Many of the onlookers thought she'd cheated. Who did this woman think she was, with her pink cannon, powered by a bicycle? What the hell? Weren't there rules against that? Any rules? She must've used some sort of explosives.

They'd never seen her in competition before. She looked so soft, like a woman with a body made out of vanilla pudding, throw pillows, or soft-serve ice cream.

Shirley was giddy. She gave Rachel a long, warm hug. The two of them had gone through a lot of trouble to be there that day. On a couple of occasions, Rachel swore her grandma was going to die before her sixty-first birthday. Shirley was sixty.

To a very careful observer, Shirley and Rachel wore the subtle scars that plague amateur inventors. Rachel's eyebrows weren't growing back as quickly as she would have liked. Shirley couldn't get the limp completely out of her leg. Her arm moved with a pinching ache.

Shirley once again peeked into the binoculars and looked through the hole in the Duster. It was a satisfying hole. The hole looked like a child monster's mouth, rimmed with jagged teeth. The orange pulp, hanging bits of seeds, and chunks of smashed rind made Shirley think of half-chewed food, strung with saliva.

Finally convinced of her personal victory, Shirley's focus through the binoculars softened. Turning around, she gently smoothed out the front of her sweater, one that she had knitted for the occasion.

Rachel subconsciously traced the faint hair of her eyebrows. Although she had been able to make them look fuller with an eyebrow pencil, she wanted her own eyebrows back.

Their launch still wasn't official.

A pickup bucked across the rutted field, stopping near the car with a fresh, new pumpkin hole in it. They looked at it how most men looked at fresh holes. At first they didn't believe their eyes.

They were used to pumpkins making serious dents in doors. They were used to pumpkins going through windshields. They were used to cheater pumpkins, loaded full of concrete. They weren't used to the fine white mist left behind from a pumpkin— quite possibly the fastest a pumpkin had ever traveled on this earth. With an expert flick of a crowbar, Sampson popped the trunk.

"Fascinating," Sampson said.

The three other men, all hunters, nodded in agreement. The result of firepower was a silent language they all understood and respected.

Sampson leaned into the trunk and fingered the sheet metal that had bent in. It was daggered. He fingered out a small ringlet of pumpkin rind. It looked like a fancy garnish used in a restaurant that served meals on china.

"I'll be…"

Still hunched over in the trunk, Sampson looked to his right. There was another hole, a bit smaller. The exit wound.

"Incredible." He cleaned his hands by rubbing them together. Small bits of wet pumpkin rolled up from them. He found the piece he'd been looking for. It was a piece of rind, marked with grease pencil. It was his handwriting and it had verified the weight of the pumpkin when it had been whole. He smelled his fingers deeply and then wiped them on his pants. He didn't smell anything hinky, like gasoline.

The scene inside the trunk, all men agreed, looked like the after-affects of a wounded animal. The tire jack in the wheel well was splattered with pumpkin guts.

Sampson sniffed inside the trunk again, concentrating. He didn't smell epoxy. The pumpkin's rind hadn't been reinforced from the outside. He was a careful, meticulous man. The trunk smelled like recently smashed pumpkin. He studied the clotted bits and the streaky bits with his eyes, nose, and fingers.

He rose up. "Looks legit to me. What do you say?"

The three men accompanying Sampson reached the same conclusion.

"Sure looks like a pumpkin," one of the men piped in. "Even though it's got a white rind, looks all the same on the inside. Orange."

The pumpkin hadn't been packed with black gunpowder and detonated upon impact. It hadn't been filled with BBs or nails. The pumpkin hadn't even been frozen. It was just a completely once-officialized, now-obliterated pumpkin. The judges had encountered all matter of tomfoolery and deceit in their four years of officiating. They were ready for anything. Hell, they knew all too well the glee that comes from satisfying explosions.

All four men looked back to the retirement-aged woman and the girl they surmised was her granddaughter in their matching bright pink sweaters, and they couldn't put two and two together. The older one looked like a crossing guard or a lady who worked at a highway tollbooth. The granddaughter was young, high school age, and her sweater was too bulky to get a reading on her development.

"She here with her husband?" one of them asked.

Sampson had checked Shirley into the competition. "No, it's just those two."

There were many support wives in the field. They served as caterers and cheerleaders, but none of them had their own launchers.

"How in the hell did she make that pumpkin cannon? She must have had help," one of the other men said.

All the others, except Sampson, nodded in agreement, figuring that cannons were a man's business.

Sampson walked away from the newly holed Duster, in the opposite direction from the firing line, in search of the last big chunk of pumpkin, the one that had made the exit hole. After a bit of searching, fifty yards beyond the Duster, he found what he was looking for. The stem. The hardest part of any pumpkin. He picked it up. It was matted with hair. He turned it around in his hands. The pumpkin had killed an unlucky field mouse and the two had fused together into a dirty, seedy, placental muck.

Sampson dropped the mouse on the ground and didn't speak of it again. The mouse was collateral damage. It hadn't been planted inside the pumpkin. He was sure of it. And although Sampson didn't know Shirley, by all forensic indications she'd thrown an honest pumpkin and that was that. Sampson looked back towards the newly holed car after he heard the familiar crack of beer cans opening. It still in the A.M. It was Saturday, and they were all volunteers.

One of the men quipped, "I believe in a balanced breakfast." His eyeballs zipped back and forth between beers. He had one in each hand. One, he instantly shotgunned. The other, he sipped. The others laughed.

When Sampson made it back to his three colleagues, he made no mention of the mouse. He held out his hand. Everyone looked at the de-moused pumpkin stem.

"That's what made the second hole?" one of them asked.

"Sure of it," Sampson said. To reinforce his statement, he pulled a long sliver of metal that was firmly lodged inside the pumpkin's flesh. "Even the paint matches."

Everyone was satisfied. Like it or not, the women had thrown a legitimate gourd.

Sampson's brow eased up. Although he trusted his friends, he didn't trust all of their friends. Sampson didn't want the kernel of doubt to sprout in people's minds, only to later flower into thorny suspicions. With any hint of wrongdoing, he knew the women's victory would be tainted with suspicion.

He looked back to Shirley. She had put on a wide-brimmed hat with a gigantic fabric rose stitched onto the front. She was carefully pouring soup from a vacuum bottle into its cap.

Sampson was also acutely aware of something that Shirley was thinking at that exact moment.

Shirley wasn't the type of person who was supposed to win this competition. She was supposed to be buying groceries somewhere, not kicking everyone's ass. Sampson liked her more and more.

Even from that distance, Sampson knew a storm of discontent was brewing.

Spittle formed at the edge of serious, long-time pumpkin

chuckers' mouths. Jaws clenched.

"This ain't right," some said.

"She cheated," another agreed.

"There's gotta be a rule against it, somewhere."

Before Sampson could jump down from the back of his pickup with his official tally sheet, a crowd had formed. He stood there for a second and cleared his throat. "I know what you're all thinking. Something ain't right."

Grumbles of agreement shot through the assembled bodies.

"I talked to…" Sampson looked at his clipboard, then found the name, "Shirley prior to the contest. She signed that she wasn't using any explosives or chemicals, just air. She didn't strike me as being the type of woman to be telling tales."

Some in the crowd guffawed and rumbled dissent.

"But, I gotta admit, sweet lord, that was one hell of a curious throw." With that, Sampson jumped out of the back of the pickup and walked towards Shirley and Rachel, who were sitting on the tailgate of the station wagon, enjoying their cider, choosing to ignore the palpable electricity generated by the disbelief that surrounded them. Shirley had planned on it. She'd warned Rachel of the possibility, too.

The man with a large mustache had pulled up a chair, introduced himself as Bocephus, and was intently, yet respectfully, prodding Shirley's knowledge of her machine.

Sampson waited for a small break in the two's conversation, then politely cut in.

Shirley looked up. Directly behind Sampson, fifty people looked directly back at her.

"Shirley? We've got to inspect your cannon for any malfeasance. We've got some doubters."

Expecting it, yet not comfortable with the attention, Shirley stammered. "S-s-s-ure. W-w-what do you want to know?"

"Might as well go through it all," Sampson replied. Nods bobbled from the crowd as it congealed around the cannon.

The next fifteen minutes were filled with a very detailed explanation of how every element on the cannon worked. Rachel thought her grandma was eloquent. Shirley explained how the flywheel turned the air compressor, how the compressor worked, and how it was extremely important to release a high volume of air all at once. She peppered her explanation with the laws of physics, ballistics, and hydraulics, much to the delight of Bocephus and the glassy-eyed stares of most of the rest of the crowd. Only two features were left out. Shirley didn't tell anyone about the rifled barrel or that Rachel had grown the special pumpkins.

"Shit, man," one whispered. "We didn't ask how she invented the fuckin' earth. Get on with it." His buddy jabbed an elbow in approval.

Shirley finished her explanation. "Any questions?"

"No propane?" one asked. "That looks like a propane tank to me."

Shirley rapped one of the tanks. "It's empty now, but it'll be filled with air before we launch."

"You did all the welding yourself," another asked.

"Yep."

"I bet you can't do it again," a cynic piped in.

"I'd love to," Shirley said.

Everybody looked at Sampson.

"You mind?" he asked.

"Not at all. Ready Rache?" Shirley asked.

"Just for demonstration. This isn't an official chuck," Sampson said, explaining to the crowd.

"My pleasure," Shirley said. "Everybody, please stand back."

Rachel pulled on her helmet and helped her grandma plunge a pumpkin down the barrel. The two women then pedaled for three minutes under watchful eyes.

Shirley hit the boat horn, hit the pressure release valve, the cannon jolted, a white flume of air shot out of the barrel, and the Duster got pegged with a fresh, new hole, two feet in front of the

184

first, right through the rear passenger door. Even from half a mile away, the hit was unmistakable as the car shivered in its suspension.

Sampson turned to the crowd. "Anybody still got a problem?"

Air was let out of the lynch mob.

"It's got tassels," someone complained again, but this time the comment got little more than a defeated snicker.

Sampson turned to Shirley. "I'm satisfied."

Sampson turned back to the crowd. "We got a whole lot more pumpkins to throw. Folks, get back to your launchers."

CHAPTER THIRTY-FIVE
The Real Win

Shirley and Rachel's second and third official launches went as planned, issuing clean hits on the faraway car.

Rachel took a break to wander through a corn maze that an adjacent farmer had set up as an attraction, then ate some pumpkin pie.

Three hours later, Sampson made his rounds and gave everyone who participated a certificate with the number of feet of each launch, inscribed in calligraphy, on a sheet of paper that was printed like an old scroll on parchment.

"It's no surprise that you won," Sampson said with a smile.

Shirley's win was official.

"What was that?" Shirley had heard Sampson, yet it pleased her to hear it from somebody else. It sure felt good.

"It's no surprise that you won."

"Thanks for letting me explain the cannon, Sampson."

Sampson hopped on his ATV, down the line to the next pumpkin chucker.

Shirley's pride—good, healthy pride of a job well done—expanded and was filled in with confidence. That fireball, that burning desire trapped inside her for so long, was no longer threatening to burn her to a crisp. It felt like it had finally come out of her and was currently levitating above her, glowing down in a spotlight of great, golden light, better than any sunset she'd ever seen. Shirley couldn't help but smile and beam. She'd frickin' done it.

Compulsively, as she had done many times through the competition, she stroked the laminated newspaper clipping of the first pumpkin chuck. It was easier for her to remember her dreams when they were always in her front pocket.

After Sampson left, Shirley turned to Rachel. "We've upped the ante."

"Face it, Grandma. You kicked their butts."

"Soundly."

Shirley—adrenaline surging through her—clinked Rachel's mug a little too roughly and Rachel's shattered. Rachel looked at the handle that was still in her hand, threw it theatrically to the ground, and jumped up and down on the broken ceramic pieces, smiling the entire time. After she was done, she collected all of the pieces and put them in a trash bag.

Late afternoon, after official competition had ended, Sampson and his helpers scooted the outhouse on the pickup truck a little bit closer to the launchers. Both Shirley and Rachel doubled over in laughter as a washing machine filled with water left a comet-like vapor trail as it was launched from an incredibly wide catapult and dead-eye landed on the outhouse, which splintered into oblivion. The crowd cheered wildly.

Still later, Rachel and Shirley gave their final salute to the day. They stuffed the pumpkin launcher's barrel full of toilet paper. After a hundred yards of flight, the rolls unfurled their two-hundred-sheet lengths and slowly fluttered to the ground.

The crowd cheered.

Shirley's reveled in the clapping and applause from scads of onlookers and fellow launchers. Her cheeks became flush and rosy.

She turned around, smiled earnestly, and waved back with both of her arms, like people do when stranded on a desert island and they see an airplane flying by.

Rachel looked at her grandma and couldn't stop smiling. Shirley had finally done it and they were both alive.

Deep down, Shirley knew she'd avoided a void. Her life: she'd finally made it something. Her own.

About the author:

Todd Taylor was managing editor of *Flipside* magazine and helped form *Razorcake*, which is now one of the top punk rock magazines in the U.S. He is the author of the widely successful book *Born to Rock*. He has published hundreds of articles, short stories, and interviews over his long career.

ALSO AVAILABLE FROM GORSKY PRESS

THE UNDERCARDS by James Jay · paperback — 100 pgs.
"This book puts the smack-down on poetry!"
   —Jim Simmerman, author of Kingdom Come

PUNCH AND PIE ed. by Felizon Vidad and Todd Taylor · paperback — 160 pgs.
"These stories are great. The corporate publishing overlords could never put out an anthology such as this."
   —The Iconoclast

BORN TO ROCK by Todd Taylor · paperback — 318 pgs.
"When Todd Taylor graces our pages, we believe in punk rock again. And punk rock gives us hope."
   —Ryan Henry, Thrasher

GLUE AND INK REBELLION by Sean Carswell · paperback — 130 pgs.
"An almost flawless collection of pure literary entertainment on the most down-to-earth, real level you could ever hope to find."
   —Jay Unidos, Maximum Rocknroll

THE SNAKE PIT BOOK by Ben Snakepit · paperback — 304 pgs.
"Ben Snakepit captures some moments and moods of our lives so well, like a great song, and when it came down to it, I couldn't resist singing along."
   —Aaron Cometbus

GURU CIGARETTES by Patricia Geary · paperback — 256 pgs.
"Patricia Geary is one of the best fantasy writers working."
   —Tim Powers, author of Last Call

BARNEY'S CREW by Sean Carswell · paperback — 237 pgs.
"Sean Carswell is a wonderful storyteller.."
   —Howard Zinn, author of A People's History of the United States

BIG LONESOME by Jim Ruland · paperback — 192 pgs.
"These stories gleam with witty mischief and an abundance of heart."
   —Mark Sarvas, The Elegant Variation

GRRRL by Jennifer Whiteford · paperback — 240 pgs.
"The novel is full of pain, laughter, music, and life."
   —John W. MacDonald, Ottawa Citizen

FOR A COMPLETE CATALOG OR TO ORDER ONLINE, VISIT:
www.gorskypress.com